Love or Money

By Elizabeth Roderick

Love or Money

Limitless Publishing, LLC
Kailua, HI 96734
www.limitlesspublishing.com

Formatting: Limitless Publishing

ISBN-13: 978-1-68058-361-8
ISBN-10: 1-68058-361-1

Dedication

For Tanna, Whisper, and all the other tough women out there making their way in this world. Our paths and stories may be different, but there can always be a happily ever after.

Chapter One

Marissa glanced over her shoulder to make sure the guards weren't looking, then pulled Riel into the bathroom.

They were alone. The only sounds were those of the sink dripping water into its stainless steel basin, and the faraway buzz of an automatic door. Riel's heart pounded as Marissa backed her up against the wall. Their hips pressed together, and their fingers intertwined.

"I wanted to give you a goodbye kiss," Marissa said softly, pressing her soft lips to Riel's.

Riel broke away and grinned mischievously. "I'd like more than just a kiss." She giggled.

Riel caught Marissa's round ass, pulling the other woman tight against her. She could feel the heat of her pussy through the thin cotton of their uniforms, and she pressed harder. A shiver ran through Riel as she felt herself get wet.

"You want something to remember me by?" Marissa asked, her brown eyes sparkling.

"Oh, yeah." Riel kissed Marissa, running her

hand down the other woman's taut, brown belly and under her waistband, finding her hard, hot clit and rubbing it slowly. "We have to be quick," she whispered. "They'll be coming back from the rec yard soon."

"Aaah," Marissa moaned, closing her eyes. "You almost got me there already, baby."

Riel rubbed harder, and Marissa's hips moved against her fingers. She slipped her other hand into Marissa's panties, making her moan again as she pushed two fingers deep inside her wet pussy.

"Riel, baby," Marissa breathed, her body moving, her fingers twining in Riel's cascade of wavy, black hair. "I'm gonna miss you."

Riel brought her lips to Marissa's, trying not to think that it might be the last time they were together like this.

Her girlfriend's soft lips parted in a gasp as Riel fucked her faster with her fingers. Marissa's eyes lit up and burned, and her pussy got hot and even wetter, her hips shuddering as she thrust hard against Riel's fingers. A small noise escaped her lips that made Riel's own clit throb.

Marissa let out a sigh and smiled, sweat dampening her smooth brow. "You want it now?" she murmured.

"Yes, Rissa. Fuck me."

Marissa kissed her slowly, dragging her fingers along Riel's thighs and sliding two of them into her wet pussy. Riel's breath caught as she felt them press deep, gently stroking her inside. "Fuck me hard, Rissa."

"You like that?" Marissa moved her fingers

2

faster, deeper, finding just the right spot inside her. In the year and a half they'd been together, Marissa had learned all the ways to make Riel come hard.

Riel moaned. "I love it. I need it. Oh, I need it so bad."

"Good, baby, 'cause I love to fuck you." Marissa pulled Riel's shirt up and ran her firm tongue around her nipples, pounding hard with her fingers. Riel gasped and moved her hips, getting close.

She felt Marissa tense up. There were footsteps approaching. Marissa's eyes darted to the door, and she pulled her fingers halfway out.

"Don't stop, Rissa, please," Riel whispered. "Oh, God, please. Make me come."

The footsteps came closer, but Marissa took one look at Riel's face and thrust her fingers in deep again. Deeper, again and again, until Riel moaned Marissa's name, trembling in ecstasy.

Marissa quickly whipped her hand out of Riel's pants just as the bathroom door opened.

Officer Cheney came in. The guard's hard gaze flicked back and forth between Marissa and Riel as they stood frozen, watching her. A drop of sweat ran down the back of Riel's neck.

Cheney raised her thin-plucked eyebrows. The radio on her belt beeped and hissed out a message garbled by static. Riel's heart pounded in her throat.

"What are you two doing in here?" Cheney asked.

"Going to the bathroom, ma'am," Marissa said, her face blank.

The guard's eyebrows crept higher, her gaze falling on Riel. "How much longer you got,

Hernandez?"

Riel's hand darted up to wipe the sweat from her nose, but she managed to hold Cheney's grey-green eyes evenly. "Just a wakeup. I get out tomorrow."

Cheney tapped her stubby fingers against her belt. "I'd be careful, if I were you. Wouldn't want to delay your release by getting in trouble."

Riel swallowed. "No, ma'am, I wouldn't want to do that."

Riel thought she saw the ghost of a smile rise to the guard's pale lips. "Get out of here, you two, if you're done *going to the bathroom*." She wrinkled her nose.

"Yes, ma'am."

Marissa and Riel let out simultaneous breaths and exchanged a relieved look as they scooted out the door.

"Good thing it wasn't Carter," Riel murmured as they power-walked down the hall to the TV room. "We'd be in the hole for sure."

"Psh," Marissa said. "Cheney would have put us there too if you weren't getting out tomorrow. Too much paperwork for no reason." Her eyes lingered on Riel's for a moment, and Riel's heart twisted at the sadness in them. "I'm gonna miss you," Marissa said.

Riel blinked back tears. "I'll miss you too." She tried to smile. "But you've only got another thirty-two months, and I'll be waiting for you."

Marissa's lips twitched into a grim smirk. She looked away at the grey-green walls. "I know you will, baby."

4

***

Riel had a hard time sleeping that night. She lay on her top bunk, listening to her roomie's familiar snore. She'd been in this place fourteen months, which seemed like a lifetime. She was lucky she hadn't gotten a longer sentence, considering the amount Isaias had her carrying when she was busted, but he'd gotten her a good lawyer.

It was hard to believe that this time tomorrow she'd be out in the wide world, able to eat and sleep whenever she wanted, go where she wanted. She thought of all the things she wanted to do on the outside—play her guitar, eat a huge plate of *carnitas*, get a pedicure, sit in the park. But when she thought of Marissa, her racing heart stumbled. And when she thought of what else was waiting for her out in the bricks, she realized that, other than the food and the pedicure, she didn't really have much to look forward to. At least in prison she'd found someone to love, and someone to love her. Outside, there was only Isaias and friends who hadn't even written to her.

Riel forced the pain from her mind. She had her sister, and she'd make new friends. Plus, she only had about two and a half years to wait for Marissa, and that wasn't long, really.

She thought of the way Marissa looked when she was fucking her. The way her body moved. She thought about her tight, wet pussy, and how she would moan when Riel found her clit with her tongue. Riel's fingers crept down inside her own panties, finding her clit and stroking it lightly. Her eyes closed, and she saw Marissa's firm, round tits. She rubbed harder, arching her back, then slid the fingers of her other hand inside herself, thrusting them deep and hard until she came with a gasp.

The fantasy drained from her mind, leaving her to stare at the light from the hall, which splashed across the concrete ceiling. She felt empty and alone. Riel curled around her pillow and eventually drifted off to sleep.

She had a horrible dream in which they'd decided to not set her free. Instead, Isaias came to live with her in her cell. He insisted on having the top bunk, and covered the walls with posters of bald eagles, muscle cars, and vapid, naked women. When Riel tried to take them down, he caught her by the wrist and slammed her into the lockers.

Riel woke with a start as the overhead lights clicked on, the glare burning through her eyelids. Her thin mattress squeaked as she flopped over and pulled her pillow over her head, craving a few more minutes' sleep before they called breakfast.

A jolt flew down her spine. This was the last time she'd be awoken by the dismal glare of fluorescent lights.

"It's Riel's last wakeup," Nora sang gruffly from the bunk below. She pounded the bottom of Riel's bunk with her heels, making the steel frame vibrate.

"Stop it, Nora!" Riel groaned.

Nora laughed. "Wake up, cutie pie, you're going home!" She stopped kicking and lumbered out of her bunk with a groan. "Goddamn, I hope they don't give me some stinky bitch for my next roomie. You've been real good to live with, and I'm going to miss you."

Riel smiled, sitting up and stretching. "I'll miss you too, Nora."

Nora blew a raspberry as she went over to her locker. "Don't waste time missing anything here. Go out and make yourself a new life. Be a good girl so you don't have to come back to this shithole."

Nora started singing "Ring of Fire" as she stripped down and put on fresh clothes. Riel couldn't keep from glancing at the other woman's tired rolls of dimpled flesh, her jiggling underarms and spider veins. Nora had been in this place for over twenty-seven years, serving a thirty-year sentence for armed robbery. In her early twenties, after her husband had died in a drunken car accident and left her with two babies, she'd fallen in with a petty crime ring just trying to make ends meet. She'd probably been beautiful when she'd first gotten to prison, but now her beauty was long gone. She'd be released a used-up old woman, long forgotten by those she'd left behind.

Riel sighed, pressing the heels of her hands into her eyes. *Make yourself a new life.* She had to try, or she'd end up like Nora, or worse.

She swung her legs over the edge of the mattress, clambered down the steel ladder, and got dressed for the last time in her prison blues.

She met Marissa in the lineup, waiting to be taken to the dining hall. Marissa had worn her hair the way Riel liked it, not straightened and tamed with clips and ponytails, but allowed to be itself, standing out big and black and frizzy in a soft halo around her head. She gave Riel a sad smile as she

7

walked up, and they clasped hands briefly when the guards weren't looking.

"Hey, baby," Marissa murmured with a slight smile. Her gaze moved away from Riel's and wandered unseeingly over the heads of the other women in line. She looked like she'd been crying.

"You okay, Rissa?"

"I'm fine."

Riel's heart clenched.

The guards took them out across the yard to the dining hall. It had been raining for weeks, but the clouds had cleared away in the night, and it looked like it would be a sunny day. The sky was pink and orange, and the early spring air was crisp and dewy. Sheets of mist swirled around the tall pines, which rose up beyond the dully gleaming loops of razor wire. Pretty soon Riel would be on the other side of that fence with those trees, and the realization sent a searing wave of adrenaline from her scalp to her toes.

Riel and Marissa got their breakfasts and sat together at one of the cafeteria tables, where some of their friends sat with them. Marissa stirred her spoon round and round in her Cream of Wheat, her eyes dull and distant. Neither she nor Riel spoke. The other women at the table chattered, filling their silence.

"I wish I was getting out today," a woman named Orla said with a wry grin at Riel. "I'd head straight to my favorite restaurant, get myself a huge plate of fried chicken and okra."

"Shit, but they ain't never gonna let you out, Orla, and it's probably a good thing."

They all laughed, except for Riel and Marissa.

After breakfast they headed back to their unit, Marissa still slump-shouldered and silent. Riel chewed on the inside of her cheek, trying to think of something to say—the magic words that would make her girlfriend feel better, that would fix everything.

But she still hadn't thought of anything when a guard approached the group, looking at his clipboard. "Gabriella Hernandez?"

Riel looked up, startled. "Yeah?"

"Come with me. Time to process your release."

Riel stood, gaping. "What, already?"

The other women looked over at her.

"Bye-bye, Riel," a girl named Lora said, rolling her eyes.

"They letting Riel out," a woman named Beatrice said with a smile. "Watch out, world."

Nora laughed and patted Riel on the back. "Good luck, honey. You be good out there."

Marissa stood frozen and wide-eyed. Riel stepped toward her, tears springing to her eyes. Marissa took her hand and quickly squeezed it once, smiling stiffly. "Go on, baby," she said. "I love you."

"I love you too," Riel said, tears spilling over.

She turned and followed the guard, looking back once as they headed toward administration. Her last glimpse of Marissa was of her girlfriend hiding her face in her hands, her shoulders shaking.

Chapter Two

Riel had to sign a mound of paperwork, and her tears kept splotching the ink.

"You're not going to miss us that much, are you?" the woman at the desk drawled.

Riel didn't respond, sniffing and drying her tears on her wrist.

The woman rolled her eyes and slid a piece of paper over the counter. "This is the information regarding your probation office. You have to report there at nine o'clock tomorrow morning, or they'll put a bench warrant out for you. So if you miss us that much, you can just come right back."

Riel stared at the sheet of paper blankly. Some women did just that: came right back, especially the ones with girlfriends. As a newly released prisoner, Riel wouldn't be allowed to visit or even write to Marissa. They'd made plans to meet up again when Marissa got out, but the realization, which Riel had been denying for months, suddenly crept in full force: it probably wasn't going to happen.

Riel bit back a fresh wave of grief. *Make*

yourself a new life. But how? It didn't even seem like she had the raw material to start with. She'd worked hard to get her GED while in prison, but Isaias had made sure she had no real work experience and no friends. Would he even allow her to get a job or her own apartment? Or would it be the same shit as before she'd been arrested?

She wiped her eyes again and took the sheet of paper about probation, following another guard down a hallway.

The guard gave Riel a bundle of street clothes her sister Lizette had brought in: a pair of jeans, her favorite red shirt. She smiled looking at them as the guard locked her in a holding cell to change. The clothes were like old friends she'd almost forgotten about. Lizette had also brought in brand new hipster panties and a cute, purple lace pushup bra. Riel put the underwear on and looked down at her body, running a finger along the cleft between her breasts. It was good to have something on besides granny underwear, to feel sexy again. Riel imagined the look on Marissa's face if her girlfriend could see her now. Marissa would put her hands inside her bra and pull her breasts free, take each nipple in her mouth, slowly slide the panties down around her ankles.

Riel sniffed and rubbed her swollen eyes, angrily pushing the thought aside.

She got dressed. The jeans were too big; they slipped down to the middle of her hips. The food had been horrible, and she'd also spent a lot of time in the gym letting off steam, so she'd been one of the few women who ended up losing weight in prison.

She sat down on the hard, wooden bench to wait. The cell was cold and windowless. She hugged her knees and watched the fluorescent lights flicker. It felt weird to be dressed in regular clothes again. She kept scratching her boobs, itchy from the lace of the bra. Every few moments, she'd remember she was about to get out and her blood would pound in her ears.

The wait seemed interminable. Her mind kept rolling over what was waiting for her on the outside, and who she was leaving behind on the inside. *Maybe I* should *come back,* she thought, but then she remembered Nora. She imagined an entire life spent within drab concrete walls, harassed by guards, immersed in petty prison drama as she slowly grew older and her life on the outside dwindled to a distant memory. She took a deep breath and straightened her shoulders. *I'm going to make it somehow. Isaias can't stop me.*

She had waited so long, so immersed in her thoughts, that it startled her when she heard the lock click and the door open. "Gabriella Hernandez?"

Riel sat up straighter. "That's me."

The guard looked up from his clipboard, his gaze immediately wandering down to her cleavage. He gave her a look she didn't like, which she'd seen on guards' faces all too often over the past fourteen months. That look said she wasn't really human. He could do anything he wanted with her, and no one would ever know or care. Each one of those looks had collected like sludge in the bottom of her soul. Would the feeling ever go away now that she was free?

The guard jerked his chin at her. "Come on, Hernandez."

He took her through a warren of bare, echoing hallways. Another guard buzzed them through a locked door, and they went out into a bright waiting room.

Sunlight streamed through the windows, making Riel blink. A tall, thin silhouette resolved itself into her sister Lizette, who was a short, slim woman with straight brown hair falling down to her butt. She had a baby in one arm—Riel's new niece, Corinne, three months old. Riel had never met her, only seen pictures. Lizette's three-year-old daughter Jessica clung to her mother's leg, watching Riel with wide, brown eyes.

Next to her sister, his beefy arms crossed over his broad chest, was Lizette's husband Isaias.

Their eyes met, and Riel's stomach clenched, bile rising into her throat. A look passed between them, a faint smile curving Isaias' lips.

Riel tore her gaze from him and rushed up to her sister, giving her an awkward hug while trying to avoid stepping on Jessica or crushing the baby. "Lizette, oh my God."

"I'm so happy you're finally out, Riel."

Riel looked up into her sister's face. She was smiling her beautiful smile, but her brown eyes were dull and ringed in dark circles. A wave of pity tugged Riel into its riptide. Being married to Isaias couldn't be easy.

Riel tickled the baby's chin. Dark hair curled over the tiny girl's forehead, and her huge, brown eyes were fringed with long, black lashes. She gave Riel a toothless grin.

"Can I hold her? Oh, she's beautiful," Riel said.

"Of course."

Riel took the baby into her arms. Corinne blinked at her, then leaned forward to suck on her chin.

Riel giggled. "Not my chin!"

Isaias shifted on his feet, sniffing. "Let's get out of this shithole. It gives me the creeps."

Riel's smile faded, and she pressed her lips together to stifle an annoyed retort. She handed the baby back to Lizette. "Okay, let's go."

They walked out the front doors into the sunlight, the balmy spring breeze catching Riel's long hair. She felt suddenly dizzy. *I'm free.*

She climbed into the backseat of the extended-cab pickup and helped her sister strap the kids in.

"Olivia's going to be so happy to see you," Lizette said. "She stayed home with Mama Maria to help get ready for the party."

"Party?" Riel asked.

"Your welcome home party," Lizette said, climbing in the front seat.

Riel grinned. "Thank you." She caught Isaias studying her over the back of his seat, and her happiness evaporated.

It was about a twenty minute drive to Lizette and Isaias' house in Portland. Traffic surrounded them in a solid, roaring stream, the houses and businesses crowding thick alongside the freeway. Isaias had some rock band on the stereo, and Lizette chattered about the party—who was coming, how they'd stayed up half the night making *tamales* and cake. The baby squawked and Jessica kicked her legs and cried that she wanted cake *now*. It was overwhelming; so noisy and normal after the snide gossip and rough banter of the other prisoners; after the stale air, bleak lighting, and press of drab prison walls, Riel felt out of place. But she gathered up her voice and spoke over the noise.

"Do you know...will Evan be there at the party?"

Isaias shot her a cruel smirk, and Lizette's bright smile faltered. "I don't know," she said. "I sent him an invitation, but I haven't talked to him."

Riel's heart sank, and she could barely listen to her sister as Lizette launched into a recitation of all the family gossip since she'd been gone. She was obviously trying to lift Riel's mood, but it wasn't working. *What do you care if Evan comes? He never wrote. He forgot about you as soon as they locked you up.*

She and Evan had never truly been boyfriend and girlfriend, but part of her had hoped they were close enough that he'd at least send her a letter now and again. That maybe he'd thought about her as much as she'd thought about him.

She hugged her knees and sighed. *Make yourself a new life.* Well, she'd have to start from scratch. She'd forget about Evan, forget about Marissa, and make an entirely new world for herself. That was, if Isaias let her. Something in the way he looked at her made her suspect he had other plans.

They pulled off I-5 and wove through the streets of the suburban neighborhood where Lizette and

Isaias lived. Riel was surprised at how unchanged it all was. There was the Thai restaurant where she'd had her first date with James Clayton, when she was fifteen. At the next intersection was the nail salon where she and Lizette used to go to have mani-pedis. And there was the Plaid Pantry where Isaias had her meet her first customer, back when he'd just had her flinging grams and eight balls.

She had changed so much in her fourteen months in custody, but in her absence the world had gone on like always.

They pulled into the tree-lined driveway of Lizette and Isaias' two-story house. Olivia, Riel's oldest niece, came running barefoot out the front door and over the manicured lawn, a little Pomeranian bounding at her heels. Isaias' mother, Maria, stood in the doorway, the thin, brown skin of her brow gathered into deep wrinkles.

Olivia skipped up to Riel as she got out of the truck and flung herself into Riel's arms. "Auntie Riel," she said.

Riel clasped her arms tight around the little girl. "Olivia! I missed you so much." The dog ran circles around them, yapping, his tongue hanging out.

Olivia took Riel's hand and started tugging her toward the house. "I'm so glad you're finally back. We got cake and a *piñata*. And I drew you a picture."

Riel let herself be pulled. Her eyes nervously met Maria's, who stood regarding her thoughtfully. Riel's heart thumped, wondering what the woman would say to her, if Maria would blame her for getting herself busted and costing so much money

16

and trouble. But instead, Maria broke into a wide smile, her gold incisor glinting in the sun.

"Welcome home, Gabriella," she said. "It's good to have you back."

Riel let out an inaudible sigh of relief, smiling back. "Thank you, Mama Maria."

If Mama Maria wasn't mad, maybe she had a fighting chance.

Riel had forgotten how warm and clean and beautiful the house was. There were vases of daffodils on the wing tables, and the mantle above the gas fireplace was lined with family photographs. It was so different from the cold prison walls that it made her dizzy.

She took off her shoes so she could feel the deep carpets and cold tile on her bare feet. She wandered around the house as Olivia chattered and showed her every drawing she'd done and toy she'd acquired since Riel had gone away.

The doorbell rang, and Riel couldn't keep her gaze from darting over as Lizette pulled the door open. She was hoping to see a tall man with dark, curly hair and bright green eyes, to see the teasing smile she'd missed so much. But it wasn't Evan. It was a short, stocky man with a kind, round face: Isaias' little brother, Andres. His girlfriend, Ashley, came in behind him.

Andres hugged Lizette. Then his gaze fell on Riel, and he grinned and strode over to her, clasping her warmly in his short arms. It struck her, as it did every time, how unlike his brother he was.

"Oh, man, it's so good to see you," he said. "You look great. Prison really agreed with you." He laughed, and Riel snorted.

He handed her the gift bag he was carrying and looked her up and down. "Seriously, it looks like you've been working out."

"Yeah, I started working out." She grinned and flexed her arms. Andres squeezed her biceps.

"Ooh, nice guns, Rielita."

Ashley looked on with her arms crossed, then stepped over, giving Riel a quick, stiff hug. "Hi, Riel. Did you learn your lesson, finally? You going to stay out of trouble?"

Riel's jaw ached from smiling. "Yeah, I learned my lesson."

"Well? What are you going to do with yourself now?" Ashley smiled too brightly, her sharp nose slightly wrinkled.

"I got my GED when I was in there," Riel said. "I'd like to go to college and get a degree in psychology." It was something she'd discussed with her prison counselor. It would be so nice, to have an education, a real job. A life of her own.

Ashley shook her blonde curls and rolled her blue eyes just slightly, shooting poison through Riel's hopeful feeling. "Do you really think they'll, like, give you a job now that you're an ex-con? I don't know if they'll even let you into college. My cousin's boyfriend couldn't so much as get a job at McDonalds because he failed the background check, and that was just for a DUI, not for dealing hardcore drugs."

Andres watched Riel's chin sag, and gave her a consoling look. "Yeah," he said, raising his eyebrows at Ashley, "but your cousin's boyfriend is

18

a dipshit, man. Riel is awesome and smart." He tousled Riel's hair and smiled, his round cheeks dimpling. He put his hand on Ashley's shoulder. "Come on, let's go say hi to my mom."

The couple went over to embrace Mama Maria just as there was another knock on the door. Riel's gaze flew over to it again, but it was Andres' sister Liliana who came in, followed by a couple of her cousins and some of Riel's friends from high school.

Forget about it, Evan's not coming, she told herself, and slouched off toward the kitchen for a soda.

Soon the house was full, and Riel was surrounded by people eating pork *tamales* and salad, congratulating her on her release with varying levels of sincerity. Most people didn't know about Isaias' business and the full circumstances of her arrest, so some of them treated her coolly, their hands guarding their wallets or clutching their purse straps tightly. Worse yet was her old high school friend, Mark, a goofy and sheltered boy who seemed to think the fact she'd been to prison lent her an aura of mystique.

"What was it like in there?" he asked, his eyes shining. "Was it like *Orange is the New Black?*"

"Never seen it," Riel said. "Sorry, I've got to go to the bathroom."

She wove through the crowd and left the kitchen, heading down the hallway. She locked herself in the bathroom, closed the lid of the toilet, and sat there with her head on her knees, breathing deeply. *Don't worry about them. Just worry about you. You aren't what they think you are, and the best way to show them that is by taking care of yourself and making the best of your life.*

It was a lonely thought, in a way; she wished she had someone else that believed in her, also. She sighed. She didn't need anyone else. She was a good person and could make it on her own.

After a while, her ears quit ringing and her stomach settled. She stood at the counter and brushed out her hair, which fell in dark brown waves to the middle of her back. *I don't look bad, for an ex-con.*

When she opened the door, she almost jumped in surprise. A tall man leaned against the wall in the hallway, his thick arms crossed over his chest. She froze, her breath catching in her throat, her heart beating frantically.

The man gave her a boyish grin, flinging dark curls out of his face. "Hey, Rielita."

"Hey, Evan." She tugged at the ends of her hair. Now that she saw him, she wasn't sure if she wanted to kiss him or punch him. *He never wrote, and he thinks he can just march back into my life with a "Hey, Rielita"?*

His green eyes searched her face, a small crease forming in his brow. Then he jerked his chin toward the back of the house. "I wanna talk to you," he said quietly.

Her hands clenched into fists. She wanted to tell him off. She wanted to give him the cold shoulder, to get back at him for abandoning her. But another part of her, the physical part, was noticing the way his broad chest filled out his t-shirt, remembering the feeling of his strong, sensitive hands on her body. And there was something else: curiosity. What did he want to say to her?

Riel chewed the inside of her cheek. "Okay. Let's talk."

She followed him into her room and shut the door, muffling the noise of the party. Lizette had made the room comfortable for her. Her bed was neatly made with her childhood teddy bear perched atop the pillows. Her guitar stood in the corner, and her fingers itched for it, even with all the other things on her mind.

Evan spent a few moments gazing at her. She stood stiffly, waiting, not trusting herself to say anything.

"I missed you," he finally said with a faint smile. "You look great."

She felt heat rise to her cheeks. She looked away, gazing unseeingly at a faded photograph of her parents on the dresser. *Don't tell him you missed him too.*

"So," he said, clearing his throat. "When's Isaias got you going back to work?"

Her eyes snapped up to his, and she crossed her arms. So *this* is what he wanted to talk about? "I'm on probation for another year. I can't even leave the county without permission until then. He'd be stupid to have me running under those circumstances."

"What, you're going to be all law-abiding now?" His full lips curled in a teasing grin. "That doesn't sound like you, Riel."

She scowled, fighting back the lump in her

throat, and she fixed her eyes back on the photograph. She could feel him studying her.

After a moment, he turned the door lock, then reached out and caught her waist, gently pulling her closer. She resisted at first, but then her will to punish him broke. His touch sent fire through her, and her body ached to be close to his, to be wrapped in his arms. She looked up at him, caught in his gaze.

"Riel, what's wrong?"

"Evan…" She huffed. What could she tell him? That she'd spent the first month in prison crying herself to sleep because he didn't write? He'd never been her boyfriend. She'd just hoped he'd cared enough.

He took her hand, stroking her palm with his thumb and frowning. She closed her eyes. His touch felt so good…

You don't need anyone else. Other people just let you down.

"Listen," he said, "I'm sorry I brought it up. I know you don't like working for Isaias. The guy's an ass to you. But it's just…I've really missed working with you."

Her heart pounded. "Evan…" She squeezed her eyes shut tighter. She wanted so badly to press up against him, feel his body against hers. Evan had almost made those long runs fun, had taught her to turn her fear and paranoia into exhilaration. They listened to loud music and giggled at funny bumper stickers. They stopped at all the best barbecue restaurants, and sometimes pulled off on lonely roads to fuck in the backseat. She remembered how his huge cock pounded deep inside her…

She stomped her foot and shrugged out of his arms, glaring at him. "Evan, you never even wrote me. You forgot about me all this time, and then you walk in here like nothing ever happened…" To her horror her voice broke, and she pressed the heels of her hands up against her eyes to stop the tears.

He didn't say anything, and for an anguished second Riel wondered if she'd scared him off, if he'd make his excuses and leave. She almost wished she could take back her words. But then she heard him suck in breath through his teeth.

"I can't believe it. You mean that dick didn't tell you?"

She wiped her eyes and looked at him. "Tell me what?"

He gazed at her uncertainly, his eyes darting to the door as if he could see through it to discover hidden listeners. "I thought he would have at least told *you*, but he must not want you to know." His eyes searched hers. "If I tell you something, you gotta promise not to say anything."

Her brow furrowed. Her hurt began to ebb, replaced by curiosity. "Of course."

He reached out tentatively and put his hand on her waist again. "Isaias told me not to write you, or accept your calls if you called me…which you didn't, by the way." He raised his eyebrows.

"Isaias wouldn't give any money to make calls, or give me people's phone numbers or anything," Riel said. "He said I'd talked to the wrong person and gotten myself snitched off, and that I'd just make it worse if I talked to them from prison, but that's bullshit. I don't know who snitched, but it wasn't you or anyone I talk to."

Evan's brow furrowed. "I thought the guy you were delivering to was the one?"

Riel shook her head. "No. I heard he got five years. He wasn't the snitch."

"Huh," Evan said. He looked thoughtful for a moment, and then he shrugged. "Well, I don't know who it was. But Isaias, like, ordered me not to talk to you, and I ended up figuring out the real reason why."

Riel frowned, her scalp prickling. "What was it?"

He reached up and brushed a lock of hair from her shoulder. "A guy I know said that Isaias cut some sort of under-the-table deal to keep you from serving an ass-ton of time in federal. Part of the deal was that we couldn't give them any reason to connect you with the organization. It had to look like you were just some small potatoes runner acting alone for your own benefit, or someone might have gotten suspicious and connected the dots. Then a lot of people would've gotten in trouble."

A chill ran down Riel's spine. "I knew he'd done something. I looked at my court papers after the plea bargain, and they said I'd only been carrying a hundred grams. I had three bricks on me when it came down. I thought that attorney he got me was just really good, and got the evidence excluded or whatever."

Evan grinned dryly. "No lawyer is that good."

Riel stood there, stunned, as Evan's fingers drew tickling patterns on her waist. "I had no idea Isaias and Maria were that well connected," she said.

"Oh yeah, they are. They don't talk about it, and that's how Maria's survived as long as she has."

"I also can't believe he'd do that for me."

Evan shrugged. "You have to take care of your own."

"Why didn't he tell me all this, then? Why let me think that you...that everyone had just forgotten about me?"

"That I don't know," Evan said. "I figured he would have at least told you."

"And why did I get busted in the first place? I spent a lot of time thinking about it, and never did figure it out."

"I don't know that either," he said. "But I'm glad you're out." Gently, with a faint, hopeful smile, he pulled her closer again. "Will you forgive me, Rielita? I would have written if I could have. I didn't want to ruin your deal and get you in trouble."

He wrapped his arms around her, and she let him. She pressed close to him, his warmth seeping into her like balm. She couldn't keep her hands from creeping up under his t-shirt, feeling the hard muscles of his back. It felt *so right* to be in his arms. She'd almost forgotten how good it was.

She grinned. "I *might* forgive you."

"Please, please forgive me." He ran his hands up her waist. "Riel, I..." He opened his mouth to say something, but then closed it again, looking a little flustered. "I like working with you," he said again.

Her heart missed a beat, and she looked up at him breathlessly. "I like working with you too,

Evan, but…"

He pulled her tighter against him, his gaze locked on hers, his eyes hazed over with longing. "But what, Rielita?"

Riel let out a breath, her words dying in her throat, and Evan bent down, bringing his lips to hers.

It felt good. She pressed into his strong arms. His tongue was slow and insistent, and his hands caressed her body, feeling all her curves. She pulled him closer, kissing him, their breaths mingling, and felt his cock getting hard against her belly.

He moved his lips down her jaw to her neck. "I missed you, Riel," he whispered, his breath tickling her skin. "I missed you a lot." His hand slid down inside the loose waistband of her jeans and squeezed her ass. "Ooh, your butt is even nicer than before," he said, laughing softly. "I guess going to prison has its upside."

She pinched the skin of his taut waist, wrinkling her nose. "You're such a jerk."

He laughed again and pushed her gently back onto the bed, crawling on top of her. "You love my jerkiness, admit it." He slid his tongue down between her breasts, his hands reaching up to grasp them. "Oh, God, Riel, you're so fucking hot. I've been counting the days until you got out."

He pulled her shirt up over her head, and she shimmied out of it. "You really would have written if he hadn't told you not to?" she asked. She gasped as he unzipped her jeans and jerked them down, his tongue finding her clit.

"Yes, but I'm a horrible writer," he said, his lips

26

moving against her pussy. "My grammar is atrocious." He kissed and licked her, and she arched her back, moving against him, her breath coming fast.

He tugged her jeans and panties all the way off, tossing them aside. He pulled her thighs apart and slipped his tongue inside her, his thumb slowly rubbing her clit.

She cried out, and he let out a muffled moan, his tongue reaching deeper, sliding in and out, his thumb rubbing harder. She ached for him, wanting him inside of her.

Seeming to hear her thoughts, he sat up and pulled off his jeans, his long, hard cock springing free. He straddled her, gazing down at her body spread out on the rumpled quilt, naked, save for the lacy pushup bra. His pupils grew large in his green eyes. "Ah, Riel, you're so beautiful." He brushed his fingers lightly down her belly, making her shiver. He pulled back the cups of her bra and sucked each of her big nipples, his fingers working their way down to her clit again.

She pressed against his hand, gasping. "Evan, I want you in me."

"Mmm. Do you? Do you want it, Rielita?" His tone was teasing, but she could hear the hoarse need behind it.

She wrapped her legs around him, digging her heels into his muscular ass and pushing him up so that the head of his cock rested against the lips of her aching pussy. She put her mouth to his ear. "I want it so bad, Evan. I haven't had a cock in me in so long."

"You sexy girl," he breathed.

He thrust himself all the way inside her, and she cried out and bucked her hips against him to get him even deeper. She slid her hands up his chest, pulling his shirt up so she could feel him against her skin.

"Oh, you're so wet," he said. "You feel so good, Riel."

She arched against him, feeling him rub against all the right places. "Ah…"

"I missed your sweet pussy," he murmured, thrusting harder. Her tits jiggled against him, and he cupped one of them and took her nipple in his mouth, biting it softly.

Pleasure took her over. He penetrated her deepest spot over and over, and she felt her pussy tighten around him, warmth spreading through her as she came. He came right after her, squeezing her tits and moaning her name.

He lay on top of her for a moment, both of them catching their breath. She liked the feeling of having him there. It was comfortable and peaceful. He smiled down at her, tracing her lips with his fingertips, and she smiled back, running her hands over his biceps.

Then he rolled off and took her in his arms, kissing her with a sigh. "I'm so glad you're back, Rielita."

She smiled and cuddled against him, pressing her cheek against his warm chest. But the real world started to seep back in, and her glow of contentment began to dissipate. She frowned, reaching up to twist one of his dark curls around her finger. "Evan…"

He gave her a searching look, then brushed his lips against hers. "I know it's not easy for you, being back."

She raised her eyebrows. "You do?"

"I know how hard it was for you, working for Isaias. You never wanted to, he made you. You never said anything, but I could see it." His jaw tightened. "I'd beat the fuck out of that guy if he and Maria wouldn't have me killed for it."

"Definitely not worth it," Riel said, feeling a jolt of fear. But it also felt good for him to say that. Did he really want to stand up for her?

A slow grin spread across his face, and he ran his fingers lightly along the curve of her waist. "I do have a way for you to get away from him, though."

They gazed at each other. Her heart sped up. "What do you mean?"

"I recently got an offer from a guy I know named Mishmash."

Her speeding heart stumbled, and she chewed the inside of her cheek. She had been hoping his plan wouldn't involve more drug running, but she should have known. "I know him. The guy down in San Diego."

"The very same. He says we can go work for him. A little more risk, maybe, because we'd have to cross the border, but it pays a lot better, and Isaias would never find us if we were down there. We could get new identities and everything so you don't have that rap following you, and to hell with that probation crap."

She took a deep breath and let it out. It would be nice to be with Evan. It would be *really* nice. But the thought of running drugs again made her feel dead inside. "I don't know, Evan." She looked up at him. "Do you really want to do this stuff for the rest of your life?"

He stroked her hair, gently working the tangles out with his fingers. "No. Not really. But…we could save up our money and retire somewhere where they'd never find us." He kissed her, his hands sliding up to play with her breasts. She kissed him back, twining her legs with his, feeling a spark of hope. Did he really want to run off with her and get a house together? Or did he just need a partner in crime?

She pulled away again and nestled against him, pressing her cheek to his chest so that he couldn't see her eyes. She didn't want him to see how she longed for the idea of living a quiet life with him, because she didn't know if he was serious, and she didn't have the courage to ask him if he meant it. It felt good just to lie in Evan's arms, to be naked next to him and feel the heat of his body. She didn't want to risk scaring him off and ruining what they *did* have by wishing they had something more.

Love is bullshit, anyway. Loving someone just leads to being hurt.

"So what do you say, Riel?" he said. "Will you come down south with me?"

"I don't know…"

His hands slowly made their way along her back to the curve of her ass. "Please come with me. We can leave tomorrow. Hell, we could leave *now*." He brought his lips to hers again, giving her a slow kiss. Then he pulled away, gazing at her. "I've missed you so much, Riel."

For a moment she thought she could see something more than his normal, flippant playfulness in his eyes, and her heartbeat accelerated. She could go away with him, away from Isaias. Maybe, if they were together, their relationship would turn into something more serious. But how long would it last before she was back in prison again, or worse? She forced herself to look away.

"I want out of this business, Evan. I got my GED, and I want to go to college."

Evan lay there in silence for a moment, then she felt him nod a bit stiffly. "I don't blame you. If I were smart like you, I'd want to go to college too."

She pinched his waist and grinned up at him. "You *are* smart."

He rolled his eyes, then fixed her with a serious look. "You really think Isaias is going to let you go to college, though?"

She swallowed. "I don't know."

Evan kissed her forehead and sighed. "Please, at least think about it," he said. "I want you to go to college too, and maybe we could set that up after a while, if you came down to work with me."

Her eyebrows shot up. "Really?"

"Yes, really, Riel." He grinned. "Maybe we could get an apartment in sunny southern California. I'd get a job at Target or something and support you while you went to college. Just normal people, all legit and shit."

Riel laughed, hoping he didn't see her hopeful blush. "I can't picture you working at Target."

"I could do it. I've got skills. I know how to help people find toilet paper and batteries."

They both broke into giggles. "Could we get a cat? I've always wanted a cat."

"Of course. We could get fifteen of them."

They giggled again, but Riel's smile faded. "In the meantime, though, we'd be running drugs."

He shrugged. "Well, it's a good way to save up money, and least you'd be away from that dick Isaias. I'd keep you safe; we'd retire as soon as we could."

She twisted a lock of her hair around her finger. "But what about Lizette and the kids? I can't leave them with him."

They exchanged a long look. Evan tried to smile. "They'd be okay, Rielita. He may not be the best husband, but he'd never hurt them. And your sister can take care of herself."

Riel's gaze dropped, and she tugged harder at her hair. She *wanted* to go, but…

Evan fidgeted with the sheets. "Will you at least think about it?" he asked.

She nodded. "I will."

"Good." He kissed her. "I'll come back to visit you tomorrow, maybe take you out to dinner or something. We can talk about it."

She grinned. "Okay."

Then they heard Olivia's voice and the patter of her feet as she came running down the hall. "Auntie Riel! Where are you?"

Riel's cheeks got hot. They jumped out of bed and started pulling their clothes on and smoothing their hair. "Coming!" Riel called.

Olivia was waiting outside the door when they emerged, her little brow furrowed. "What were you doing in there?"

Evan grinned and ruffled the little girl's dark hair. "I just wanted to talk to your auntie. I haven't seen her in a long time."

Riel shuffled her feet as Evan glanced at her with a smirk.

"Oh," Olivia said, looking back and forth between the two of them. Then she broke into a bright smile and took Riel's hand, pulling her down the hallway. "Well, come on, it's time for cake."

As the three of them walked into the very crowded kitchen, Riel caught Isaias giving her and Evan a long, thoughtful glance. She looked away, smiling at her sister, who was holding out the knife for her to cut the cake.

The crowd parted, and she approached the table. The cake was huge, piled high with orange and pink frosting roses, and had '*Felicitaciones,* **Gabriella**' written on it in looping, purple script. As Riel sank the knife into it, the crowd erupted in cheers, and several arms reached out to pat her on the back.

Maria stood at her elbow, her gold tooth glinting as she grinned. "*Bienvenida a casa,*" she said as Riel handed her a slice. "We're glad to have you back."

"I'm glad to be back, Mama Maria," Riel replied. She forced a smile, feeling Isaias' eyes still on her.

Chapter Three

It was almost midnight before the party finally broke up. Riel didn't get another chance to speak to Evan alone—she felt like Isaias was watching them, and it had made her nervous—but he'd given her a significant look and blown her a kiss as he'd headed out the door. She watched him go, wondering if she should take him up on his offer.

But taking off for SoCal to run cross-border for Mishmash, whom she barely knew, made her more than uneasy. If she hadn't had her sister and nieces to think about, she might risk it without much thought. But she had no idea if she'd be walking into a worse situation than she had at Isaias'. There would be no coming back to Isaias if she left, no guarantee she could ever see her sister and nieces ever again, and they were her only remaining family.

It would be nice to be with Evan, though. She felt warm and happy as she helped her sister clean up paper plates and plastic cups.

But would it? Did he really care about her, or

would he lose interest, abandoning her in a bad situation amongst strangers?

"You and Evan were sure making eyes at each other," Lizette said, shooting Riel a sly smile as she wiped down the table. "Is there something going on there?"

Riel rose guiltily out of her thoughts and threw a wadded napkin at her sister, her face burning. "Stop it, Lizette."

Lizette giggled, picking up the fallen napkin. "Well? It's obvious, right? You two have it bad for one another."

Riel hid her face behind her hair. "I don't know if he really likes me that way."

"Oh, whatever," Lizette said as she waved a hand at Riel dismissively.

Lizette continued to wipe down the counters, and Riel looked closely at her. There was a furrow that never quite left her brow, and her face was pale and too thin.

"Are you okay, Lizzy?" she asked.

Lizette looked up, blinking. "Yeah. Why?"

"Everything been okay here while I was gone?"

"Of course." Lizette smiled, but Riel thought she could see the strain behind it. She dropped her rag and pulled Riel into a hug, where Riel laid her ear against her chest the way she used to as a little girl.

"I missed you, Lizzy."

Lizette stroked her hair. "I missed you too."

Riel stood there for a moment, just listening to her sister's heartbeat, feeling eight years old again. But she wasn't eight years old anymore; she had to take care of herself and her family, make the right decisions, and be an adult. She looked up into her sister's sad, brown eyes. "What do you think would have happened if Mama and Papa hadn't died?"

Lizette was silent for a moment and then shrugged jerkily. "I don't know Riel," she said quietly, pulling away and running a hand through her hair.

"I think we would have both gone to college. You could have gone to art school, like you wanted."

Lizette shifted on her feet, a pained look crossing her face. She smiled. "I wish they hadn't died, but I can't complain about my life. I have a good husband and kids, a nice house."

Riel opened her mouth to say something about that, but she stopped herself as she heard footsteps approaching from the hallway. Lizette's smile faltered, and she stiffened.

Isaias came in and leaned against the doorjamb, jerking his chin at Lizette. "Why don't you get some rest, Lizzy? It looks like you've got everything cleaned up pretty well."

Lizette twisted the dishrag between her hands, then set it down on the counter. "Okay." She kissed Riel's forehead and headed off to her bedroom.

Riel stood where she was, watching Isaias warily as he went to the fridge for a beer. He seated himself at the kitchen table, then pushed out the chair next to him with his foot and grinned. "Sit down, Rielita. I haven't even had a chance to talk to you yet."

Riel lowered herself into the chair, her foot nervously bouncing up and down. Isaias twisted the cap off the beer, his brown eyes wandering over her face and body. "It's right, what they all say. You look good. Even better than before."

He tipped back his beer as she twisted her hands together in her lap. "Thank you," she said.

He set the empty bottle down on the table. "You give any thought yet about how you're going to pay us back for the three bricks you lost us, and the lawyer fees?"

She clutched her knees. "I'm sorry that happened, Isaias, but it wasn't my fault."

"Then whose fault do you think it was?"

Riel gritted her teeth, glaring at him. "I don't know what happened. I don't know who tipped the cops off, but it wasn't me. I did everything just the way you told me, and didn't talk to anyone about it."

He ran a hand over his short, brown hair, his nostrils flaring as he sighed. "Well, you did something, Riel, and it cost us a lot of money, whatever it was. But don't worry, I'm not mad at you. I know you'll make it right."

She dug her fingernails into her knees. "Cut the bullshit, Isaias. What do you want?"

He pulled a mock serious face, pursing his lips. "Tsk, tsk. Prison's given you a dirty mouth, little girl. Is that any way to treat the man who's keeping you off the streets?"

"I don't need you. I only came back here because of Lizette."

His lips pulled into a cruel grin. "You think you don't need me? What do you think would happen to you out there, Riel? If they didn't haul your ass

37

straight back to jail for violating your probation by not living in your approved residence, then the wolves would split a cute little thing like you straight down the middle before the sun was up."

"I'd find someplace else. I'd get a job." But she could barely meet his eyes. A void of hopelessness opened in her stomach. He laughed.

"Sure you would. Easy for a nineteen-year-old high school dropout just out of prison to get a job, right? Especially a job that earns you enough to pay rent and bills all by yourself. "

"I got my GED, and I have other people who would take me in."

That made him laugh harder. "Who'd take you in? Evan? He your little boyfriend now, Rielita? Some big man he is. I had a little chat with him, and he ran away like a scared puppy, pissing down his leg. You won't be seeing him any time soon. I guess he didn't think you were special enough to fight for."

She felt like he'd punched the air out of her lungs. Had Evan really run away? Tears rose to her eyes, and it just made it worse that Isaias could see them there. She wanted to scratch the look of triumph off of his face.

"Face it, Riel," Isaias said. "You need me. You would have been fucked without me before you got busted, and you'd be even worse off without me now."

She stared at her lap, pressing her lips together to hold back the sobs and the screams. She *hated* him. She hated him so bad that she had to clutch the seat of her chair to keep from punching him in his smug, asshole face. But she had to hold it together. She had to find a way out of this somehow, and she wouldn't get anywhere by pissing him off worse. She swallowed hard, forcing her anger into a hard knot in her chest. "What do you want with me?"

"Don't worry, I'm not going to put you back running again. You've proven you're not capable."

Riel huffed, but held her tongue.

"Besides," he continued, leering, "I think you're more valuable to me elsewhere now that you're legal age and starting to fill out a bit."

Riel's shoulders tensed. Her heart took off running. "What do you mean?"

"I bought a club while you were away. It's a nice little business, brings in a fair amount of money." His leering grin grew wider, and he reached out with his sock-clad foot to nudge her calf. "You know how to dance, right?"

Before she could stop herself, she jerked away from him, her chair legs squeaking on the floor tiles. "Nuh-uh. No way. I'm not dancing in a titty bar."

"Oh, come off it, Riel. You'll be popular there if you loosen up a bit. You're not the scrawny little kid you used to be. You're actually turning out pretty hot."

Riel crossed her arms, taking a deep breath through her nose and letting it out, willing herself not to explode. "*No*, Isaias."

"No? Then what are you going to do to pay me back, Riel?" He raised his socked foot and ran his big toe slowly along the back of her calf.

Her spine stiffened. "Stop it, Isaias."

He laughed softly, and the toe's progress halted. He put his foot back on the ground. But then he leaned forward and reached out to squeeze her knee. "You don't call the shots in my house, Rielita." He dragged his fingers along the inside of her thigh. "I pay for the roof over your head and everything else, plus I saved your ass from a thirty-year sentence. You wouldn't have a life at all if it weren't for me, and this is how you treat me?"

She squeezed her eyes shut, bile rising into her throat. "Stop, Isaias. I won't do this...I won't do that to my sister."

"Your sister won't know what we don't tell her." His fingers made their way up to her crotch, and he pressed them hard against her pussy through the fabric of her jeans. Then he leaned closer, taking her earlobe between his teeth, and his other hand slid under her t-shirt to cup her breast. Riel squeezed her eyes shut, fighting back her nausea and frantically trying to think of a way out of this trap.

"In fact," Isaias murmured, "I think I'll take my payment both ways. I'll pound your hot cunt, *and* I'll see you up there on stage, wiggling around for tips."

Panic took hold of her, and she pushed herself away. She tried to spring up from her chair, but he caught her wrist and yanked her back down, hard enough to make her cry out in pain.

"Where do you think you're going?"

"Isaias, I—"

"You think you can fuck with me, Riel?" He twisted her wrist, and she yelped again. "I work my fucking ass off for you and your goddamn sister, and I'm not going to take any shit from you."

Then Maria's voice broke through the struggle. "Isaias!"

He froze, and so did Riel. Mama Maria came in, her long, grey hair hanging down her back, her flannel nightgown falling to her thick calves. She fixed hard eyes on her son. "*Sueltala!*"

He glared angrily at his mother, but he let Riel go. Riel stepped back from him, massaging her wrist.

Maria's emotionless gaze fell on Riel. "Riel, we give you a good home. You need to follow the rules. You'll go to work, like he says." She looked back at her son, anger flashing in her eyes. "And Isaias, stop breaking fucking commandments. God will punish you."

Isaias stared a challenge at his mother, his mouth tight, but he didn't say anything.

"Go to bed, both of you," Maria ordered.

Riel didn't wait to be told twice. She ran down the hallway and locked herself in her room, then sat on her bed with her face on her knees, trembling. *I'd rather be back in prison than dealing with this shit.*

She sat for a long time, letting her heartbeat slow down. She didn't know what to do. She didn't see how she was going to get out of this with her life and her dignity intact. But she'd find a way. There was no way she was going to let Isaias be the boss of her forever.

If Evan came back at that moment, Riel knew she'd leave with him. She remembered his arms

41

around her, his cock in her, his sweet words and caressing hands. Had he really abandoned her? Were a few threats from Isaias enough to make him forget his promises? Her heart squeezed, and a fresh wave of tears sprung hot into her eyes.

With great effort, she forced them back. Thinking about all this stuff wasn't going to help her right now. If Evan kept their dinner date for the next day, then good. If not, there was nothing she could do about it, and there was no use crying. She sat up and picked up her guitar, testing the suppleness of the strings.

As she played, working out a song she'd had in her head, her muscles loosened, her pain and fear eased. *I'll find some way out of this. I just have to keep my eyes open and not lose hope.*

Her fingers were soft and out of practice, but she played until she couldn't keep her eyes open any longer. She set the instrument aside and went to sleep.

Chapter Four

Riel was startled awake by the sound of Jessica yelling wordlessly as she pattered down the hall. Riel lay blinking for a moment, confused about where she was.

She remembered, and warmth bloomed in her. *I'm out.*

But memories of the night before poured in, twisting her guts into knots. *I'm in Isaias' house.*

The smell of cooking sausage wafted under the door, and her stomach rumbled. As much as she loathed the thought of facing her brother-in-law, she'd have to get up sometime. She hauled herself out of bed and pulled on some clothes, then padded out of the room and down the hall to the kitchen.

Lizette stood at the stove, Jessica tugging at her bathrobe and squawking. Olivia was bouncing the baby over by the kitchen window.

Isaias and Mama Maria sat at the kitchen table. Both of them looked up when Riel walked in. Maria smiled and pushed out a chair for her. "Good morning, Rielita. Sit down."

43

Lizette turned and smiled, but Riel was caught in Isaias' burning glare; he hardly noticed his wife. As Riel took her seat, his lips curled into a slow grin.

"Here she is, little Rielita," he said. "Now the whole family is finally together."

He kicked back in his chair, smirking at her, and Riel tore her eyes away. Lizette put a plate of sausage and eggs in front of her. Her sister looked even more worn out than she had the night before.

Riel ate in silence, listening to Olivia's lively chatter. She kept her eyes on her food, but she could feel Isaias glancing at her, his presence like a looming shadow. It wasn't until Lizette began clearing away the plates that he spoke again.

"Get cleaned up, Rielita." He pushed himself back from the table. "We've got to go in about an hour."

She looked up at him sharply. "You're the one taking me to check-in with probation? I thought…" She glanced at Lizette, who avoided her eyes, busying herself with the dishes.

"I'm taking you," Isaias said. "After that, we're going to work."

Riel's breakfast went sour in her stomach. Lizette turned to look at her, clutching a dirty plate in her hand, but quickly turned away when Isaias sent her a glance.

Maria smiled. "Go make yourself pretty, Gabriella. You're going to make a lot of money for the family."

Riel sat woodenly for a moment, but eventually stood up. "Yes, Mama Maria," she said.

She stalked down the hall and into the bathroom,

slamming the door and leaning her forehead on the cool tile of the countertop. The idea of dancing naked for a bunch of drunk assholes made her want to bash her head until she was unconscious.

She needed out. Why hadn't she just gone with Evan the night before? Whatever working for Mishmash was like, it had to be better than this.

Would she be back in time tonight, if Evan did actually decide to show up?

She took a deep breath and let it out. There was nothing she could do about it. She didn't have Evan's number; she didn't even have a phone. If he really cared about her, he'd show up and wait for her.

And what would Isaias do about it, if he did? Mama Maria would beat her son down if he tried to hurt Evan, wouldn't she? At least, unless she knew he was planning to leave with Riel...if Mama Maria found that out, there'd be trouble.

Riel turned on the shower and let the water get hot, which filled the bathroom up with billowing steam before she stepped in.

It had been so long since she'd had a *real* shower, not the lukewarm drip that passed for one in prison. Other women had always harassed her into hurrying up or asked to borrow her conditioner.

She took a long time lathering shampoo and conditioner through her thick hair, soaping every inch of herself, letting the water run over her body, which eased the tightness out of her muscles. By the time she got out and wrapped herself in a soft towel, the bathroom was so full of steam she could barely see the far wall.

Isaias was waiting by the door tapping his foot by the time she was dressed and ready. He raised his eyebrows when he saw her. "That's all the makeup you're wearing? You look like a well-endowed fifteen-year-old." He grinned. "Never mind. It could work."

Riel followed him out of the house through the misty rain, cursing under her breath.

She climbed into the cab of his truck, hunching as close against the passenger door as she could. She stared at the water beading on the windows, ignoring Isaias as he climbed into the driver's seat. He started the engine and turned off the radio. They pulled out of the driveway in complete silence, save for the sound of the heater blowing and the rain hissing on the truck's roof.

Riel could feel him glancing at her. Finally, he blew out a long breath through puffed cheeks. "Listen, Riel. I know you're pissed off at me, but there's no reason to be like this. I'm trying to take care of you."

She glanced over at him, crossing her arms.

"Whatever, be that way then," he said. "Listen, when you talk to your probation officer, tell him I have you working in the offices of Zuniga Enterprises doing filing and payroll, stuff like that."

She scowled. "If this dance club of yours is supposedly a legitimate business, why can't I tell the truth?"

He snickered. "You tell him you're gyrating in some titty bar, I'm sure he'll make some excuse to come check that out, just to make sure everything's on the up-and-up, that you're not getting drunk on

46

the job or doing anything shady. But once he sees those hot, round breasteses jiggling around up there, he's going to get ideas. Do you really want to end up giving your probation officer a lap dance or worse in exchange for staying out of jail?"

He glanced between her and the road, raising an eyebrow, until she finally looked away. She crossed her arms. "Okay, fine. I'll tell him I'm working in the office."

"*Bueno.* Good girl." He continued to glance at her with the smirk she always had the urge to burn off with a flamethrower. She tried not to look at him, but it was maddening, and she couldn't keep her eyes from sliding over to his.

"Come on, Rielita," he said. "Don't be this way. It won't be so bad working with me in the bar. I'm a nice guy if you get to know me."

Riel bit back all the insults she wanted to hurl. It would just make life harder if she fought him, and it might even make it easier if she didn't. He might let his guard down.

She swallowed the sour taste in her mouth and tried to keep the contempt out of her voice. "I'm sorry, Isaias," she said. "I just, you know, feel weird about all this. Getting out, being back in the real world again, it's strange. And now having this job. I've never done anything like that. I don't even know how to dance."

He grinned. "The dancing isn't the important part." He reached out and pinched her waist. She flinched but kept herself from jerking away. "Don't worry about that stuff," he said. "I'll always take care of you, as long as you're a good girl and do the

47

right thing, okay?"

"Okay." She forced a smile. It felt more like a grimace, but he must have believed it because he pinched her waist again.

***

He dropped her off on the fringes of downtown, in front of a squat, four-story building. "Text me when you get out of there, I'll come get you," he said.

Her brow furrowed. "I don't have a phone yet."

He smacked himself on his forehead. "Oh yeah, I forgot." He fished in his coat pocket, pulled out what looked like a brand new Motorola cell phone, and handed it to her. "All yours. I meant to give it to you this morning. I'm in the contacts, so yeah. Text me when you get out."

She looked down at the phone and turned it over in her hands, wondering what the catch was. "Thanks, Isaias."

He grinned. "No problem."

He pulled away and she stood there in the misty drizzle, gathering courage to go in. It still felt strange, to be out here alone on the sidewalk, outside of prison walls and free to go wherever she wanted.

Although she wasn't really free. How could she think that things would have changed when she got out? Isaias kept her on a tight rein like always, and it would be easier for him than it ever had been before. Now she was an ex-con, subject to strict probation requirements, and scorned by polite

48

society. Ashley was right; no one would give her a job with a prison record. They probably wouldn't let her into college, either.

Why didn't I just leave with Evan yesterday? I could have sent word back to Lizette somehow, gotten her out of there. Maybe Evan would keep his promise and come back tonight. Would he want to risk fighting Isaias over her? Or had he just wanted someone to fuck on those long cross-border runs, and now he'd find someone else with less baggage?

A man with hunched shoulders and a scraggly beard came out of the building. He flipped up the dirty hood of his raincoat, staring blatantly at her as he strutted down the sidewalk. Riel watched the torn hems of his jeans catch under his heels as he sloshed through the puddles. *I'm a loser now, an ex-con, just like that guy probably is.*

She sighed and forced the thought away. *I'm going to figure some way out of this.* She squared her shoulders and headed up the steps to the front entrance.

Her first appointment wasn't so bad. They made her do an observed urine screen; she had to piss in a cup while a block-shaped woman stood over her, looking like a pillow shoved in a tight rayon case. But Riel had endured worse in prison.

Her probation officer was a harried looking white guy named Carl Macias. His brown hair kept falling out of his comb-over. He pushed a lock of it off of his pasty, wrinkled forehead as he read through her paperwork.

"Hundred grams, huh?" he said, then grinned humorlessly. "Pretty good for a first offense."

Riel wrinkled her nose. He didn't know the half of it. "Yeah," she muttered, staring at her lap. She heard Carl flipping through the papers.

"But you say here you've never done drugs."

"No." It wasn't exactly the truth—she'd smoked pot a couple of times with Evan and even tried coke once, but she hadn't liked any of it, and it would just complicate things if she mentioned it.

"Eighteen years old, delivering coke, and you didn't even have any sort of habit to feed," he said. "Why did you do it?"

"For…for the money."

Carl's eyes dropped back to the paperwork. "Your parents are dead?"

"Yeah."

"How did that happen?"

Riel winced. "Crossing the desert. They were deported and were trying to get back to me and my sister, but they ran out of water or something I guess." She swallowed hard.

"You're a citizen, though. Born in Seattle."

"Yeah."

"How old were you when they died?"

"Ten."

Carl gazed at her for a moment, but she couldn't read his look. "I'm not going to order you to go to drug treatment right now," he said. "You'll have random testing, and as long as you come up clean and keep a job, you keep me happy, okay?"

She tried to smile. "Thanks."

***

She texted Isaias as she left the office, and about five minutes later he pulled up to the curb. She jumped back to keep from being splashed with muddy water from the gutter, but some still got on her shoes, soaking them through. She cursed Isaias under her breath.

She climbed into the passenger seat, pulling her hands out of the sleeves of her sweater and holding them in front of the heater vent. Her hair laid in a damp mass down her back, and her toes were freezing inside her wet sneakers. She wondered where her raincoat had gone. She hadn't found it in her closet. *Maybe Isaias threw it away, just to make my life more miserable.*

"You ready to go to work, little girl?" Isaias asked.

She shrugged, dislodging a drop of moisture that ran down her spine.

"That's the spirit," he said, rolling his eyes.

The club hadn't opened yet. The only person there was a young, muscular guy behind the bar counting money. He smiled at them as they came in, his friendly eyes lingering on Riel. "Hey, Isaias!" he said.

"Hey, Robert." Isaias put his hand on Riel's shoulder, and she stiffened. "This is my sister-in-law, Riel, who I told you about."

Robert trotted out from behind the bar to shake her hand, his biceps straining against the cuff of his t-shirt. "Hey, nice to meet you, Riel."

She smiled at him, and he ended up shaking her hand for a long time, until Isaias cleared his throat.

Robert dropped her hand and ran his palm over

his short-cropped brown hair, looking sheepish. "You starting today?" he asked.

"Yeah," Isaias said, answering for her. "When's Laina going to be here?"

"She usually gets here in about fifteen minutes," he said.

"All right, thanks, Robert. When she gets in, tell her I want to talk to her." He glanced sideways at Riel. "Come to the back with me, let's go over some things."

Riel followed him through to the back. The club was a large, long building with a big stage right in front, two small stages on either side, and there was an octagonal bar in the very center of the room. It smelled like ancient spilled booze and Pine Sol, but she figured it could smell much worse.

They went down a hallway behind one of the small stages. Isaias flipped a light on, illuminating black-painted walls lined with old-fashioned pinup posters. He unlocked a door and led her into a large, neat office.

He shut the door and stretched out in a leather chair behind his glass-topped desk, folding his hands behind his head. Riel stood, twisting her fingers together in front of her.

"Sit down," he said. "Jesus, Riel, you look like I'm going to bite you."

She eased herself into an armchair facing him.

"That's better," he said. "What kind of bug do you got up your butt? It's not poisonous, is it? Do I need to take you to the doctor?"

She just rolled her eyes and looked at him expectantly.

He rolled his eyes in response and leaned forward. "Okay. This is what's going to happen. You'll work here four days a week. Anyone asks, you're getting paid minimum wage plus twenty-five percent of your tips, but in reality most of that money is going to come back to me, to pay what you owe. I will give you ten percent of your tips, though, as cash, for you to use."

Riel gripped the armrests of her chair. She drew a breath, but had to press her lips shut against the words she wanted to hurl at him. *It won't help to get mad. It will just make things worse.* She let the breath out. "Ten percent?" she said through clenched teeth.

"Hey, it could be good money. Some of the girls here bring in over a thousand a day in tips. You'll have to get over yourself a bit if you want to make that much, though. Being hot isn't everything."

She pounded her fists on her thighs, her anger surging up her throat like vomit. "Isaias, I'm not going to work in this shithole and not even get paid anything!"

All traces of joviality drained from his face, and his smile grew sharp. "You'll do what I tell you, Rielita. Besides, what do you need money for? I give you everything already. A roof over your head and three hot meals a day, and all you can do is bitch about it."

Riel hid her face in her hands, her ears ringing. If Isaias really had driven Evan off, she'd need money in order to escape. But it would take her forever to save up if she was only getting ten percent of her tips. And, knowing Isaias, he'd probably figure out some way to take that away from her too.

But there was nothing she could do. Fighting wouldn't get her anywhere. She made herself relax, forcing the lump out of her throat. Riel's anger drained away. It was a self-preservation technique she'd perfected in prison, when guards or long-timer bitches would get up in her shit, trying to goad her into a fight. *I'll figure out something. I'll get out of here, one way or another, and then I'll show this dick what's what.*

She didn't see how, though. Hopelessness bit at her insides. She pulled her hands away from her face, making herself look at her captor. She shrugged. "Okay, Isaias, whatever."

"That's more like it."

There was a knock on the door, which made Riel's taut nerves tighten.

"Come in," Isaias called.

The door opened, and a young woman stepped in, black leggings hugging the pert curves of her ass. She was tall and thin, a curtain of silvery blonde hair falling to the middle of her back. "You wanted to see me?"

"Laina!" Isaias said, grinning. "This is my sister-in-law, Riel. She's starting work here today, and I need you to train her."

Laina's expression didn't change as her ice-blue eyes looked Riel over. She nodded once.

"Cool," Isaias said, leaning back and putting his hands behind his head again. "You two go off and do that. I want Riel on when we open; give her a chance to get used to it before the place fills up."

He spun away in his chair with an air of

dismissal. Crossing her arms tight over her middle, Riel stood up and followed Laina out the door.

Laina waited in the hallway, her eyes gleaming in the dim light. She had a porcelain-pale, heart-shaped face, beautiful but cold; Riel searched it fruitlessly for some sign of emotion. "Let's go to the dressing room," Laina said.

Riel nodded. They went down the hallway and through a black-painted door marked "Private" at the very end. Inside, it was pitch-black and windowless. Laina flipped a switch, and a ceiling lamp clicked on, casting its dirty glow on racks of clothing, where stuff was draped haphazardly and piled in heaps beneath. There were short skirts and little superhero capes, veils and nunchucks. A vanity with a large mirror stood against the far wall, and a faded and stained sofa sat across from it.

Laina closed the door and stood gazing at Riel again.

"You're Isaias' sister-in-law," she said. Her lips were painted bright red, and Riel watched them in fascination as Laina talked. "I don't know how much he's already told you about how we do things here."

She spat the words out like an accusation, and Riel's eyebrows drew together. She shook her head. "Nothing. He hasn't told me anything at all."

Laina's expression didn't change, but Riel saw something kindle in her eyes—curiosity, it looked like, and disbelief. "Well, the rules are pretty simple," Laina said. "Make the customers horny. Get them to request lap dances...or whatever else." Her red lips quirked slightly, the curiosity in her gaze burning brighter, to the point where an unspoken question hovered between them.

"What do you mean, *whatever else*? What else is there?"

Laina raised a thin, penciled eyebrow, her eyes icing over again. "I don't get it," she said.

"Well, that makes two of us," Riel said, crossing her arms.

"Did Isaias send you to play dumb and spy on us? Because that's not going to work."

Riel opened her mouth, but her planned retort died in her throat. She didn't know what she'd expected Laina to say, but it hadn't been that. "*Spy on you?*" She saw a flicker of fear in the other woman's eyes, which darted toward the door nervously, as if to make sure it was still closed. Riel realized she'd yelled, and lowered her voice to a murmur, even though her temper was threatening to blow the top of her head off. "Listen. I wouldn't spy for Isaias even if he paid me. But he's not paying me shit, he's only giving me ten percent of my tips. That's not enough to put up with you acting like some sort of ice queen toward me and accusing me of *spying*, and it's sure as hell not enough to pay for *whatever else* horny drunk men might want from me. I don't know what's going on with that, or what I did to make you personally hate me, but all this is *bullshit.*"

Riel realized she had tears in her eyes, and blinked them away furiously. It wasn't even noon yet, and she was already exhausted.

Laina stood looking startled. "I didn't…Riel, don't cry, I'm sorry."

"I'm not crying," she insisted angrily, her voice thick. Tears streamed down her face, and she wiped them on the sleeves of her sweater.

Then she looked at Laina, whose red lips were screwed up as she tried to hold back a laugh. Something in Riel loosened at that look, and a giggle broke through her tears. "Okay, I am crying, actually," she said.

"I didn't mean to be an ice queen," Laina said. "I just thought..."

"You just thought I was stupid enough or a big enough vag to spy for that asshole." She fought back the ache in her chest. She was so *done* with Isaias, and all of this.

Laina's expression seemed to melt. "Come here," she said as she held out her arms, and before Riel knew quite what was happening she was sobbing with her cheek on the other woman's soft breasts. Laina smelled like spicy musk, and her hands were soft as she traced gentle lines down Riel's spine.

"Are you serious, that he's only paying you ten percent of your tips?" Laina asked.

Riel nodded. She didn't care who knew about her situation. She didn't care about anything right now. "He's such a dick," she said.

"Hmph," Laina said dryly. "That's the truth. But why are you working here then? I mean...I know it's none of my business..."

Riel sniffed. "He says if I don't do everything he says, he's going to kick me out. And right now, I don't have anywhere else to go." She fought back a fresh wave of sobs. *Evan, please don't listen to*

Isaias' bullshit...please come back tonight.

Laina was silent for a moment, her fingers playing with Riel's hair. "Yeah, that sounds like Isaias, all right," she murmured.

Riel looked up at her. She was staring off at nothing, a crease in her pale brow, but when she caught Riel looking, the perturbed expression vanished and she smiled. It wasn't a very convincing smile, but it was the first one Riel had seen from her, and it made her pretty in a very different way. Riel's heart beat a little faster, suddenly aware that their bodies were pressed close together.

Laina tucked a lock of Riel's hair behind her ear. "I'm sorry I accused you of being a spy."

"It's okay," Riel said, a little breathlessly. "I am his sister-in-law, I can see why you wouldn't trust me."

Laina gazed at her distantly. Riel wondered what she was like under the shell, if there was some hot emotion beneath it. Laina held Riel's gaze long enough to make her obsess over the closeness of those red lips, then Laina blinked and looked away, trying to smile again, a tinge of color rising to her cheeks.

"Well, you may not want to be here, but you are, so I guess I should show you the ropes."

She pulled away gently, leaving Riel feeling cold and alone again. Riel wrapped her arms around herself. "Yeah, I guess so."

Their eyes met again, and Laina gave her a dark look. "We won't talk about the *whatever else* right now. If Isaias didn't tell you, then I'm not going to."

Riel's stomach curdled. "I take it there's more going on in this place than just dancing."

Laina nodded, her eyes drifting to the corners of the room. "Maybe Isaias has enough class not to get his sister-in-law involved in stuff like that."

Riel snorted. "If he has any class at all, I don't know what dark orifice he's been hiding it in." She felt suddenly ill, and Laina seemed to notice. She laid a delicate hand on Riel's shoulder, and her skin tingled.

"Don't worry about it, forget I said anything." Laina's blue eyes scanned her face. "How old are you, anyway?"

"Nineteen."

She smiled faintly. "Sorry, but you don't look it." Her eyes crept down a bit before snapping back up. "Not in your face, anyway. Let's put some makeup on you to make you look older. I'll be damned if we'll throw you to the bad creepers on your first day."

Riel sat down at the vanity, which was spread out with makeup, but Laina went over to a locker in the corner and got out a purse. "Don't use that stuff," she said, wrinkling her nose at the stuff on the vanity as she dug around in her bag. "I have some. You're not supposed to share makeup, but I don't mind sharing with you, if you don't."

Riel's gaze lingered over the perfect skin of Laina's face, wondering if the rest of her body was just as smooth. "Not at all."

She closed her eyes while Laina painted them, enjoying the feeling of her delicate hands brushing against her skin.

"The customers don't get to touch you while you're onstage, or even when you give them lap dances," Laina said. "That's the most important thing. There will be bouncers watching, and they'll help you out if you need it."

"How often do you need it?" Riel asked.

"Not as often as you'd think. The guys forget themselves sometimes, and you have to remind them. But most of the guys learn quick that they'll get kicked out for good if they break the rules. Besides, they know if they pay a bit more…"

"…they get *whatever else*," Riel muttered.

Riel still had her eyes closed and couldn't see the answer on Laina's face, but she heard it well enough in her silence. Her hands balled into fists, wishing she could tear Isaias' head clean off, praying again that Evan would come to get her or that she could figure another way out of this mess before she ended up having to prostitute herself.

Chapter Five

Music thumped through the club loud enough to make the stage lights vibrate. Riel danced, or tried to; she had never done much dancing, especially in heels. But, like Isaias and Laina had said, the dancing wasn't really what mattered, especially on the side stages. Riel quickly discovered it was more how you interacted with the customers.

There were four men clustered up against her stage now, and Riel leaned forward a bit, shaking her bare tits in front of one of them. Being naked in public was actually a little bit fun. It felt liberating. And it was interesting to watch men's reactions to her, as long as they followed the rules and kept their hands off. Which they had, so far.

She smiled at the guy in front of her, who had a bad haircut and even worse mustache. He held a drink in one hand and clutched a dollar bill in his other, watching her jiggle with glazed-over eyes. "You're new here, aren't ya, sweetie?" His eyes never left her boobs.

"Yeah," Riel said. "Just started today."

He reached out and slid the dollar bill between her spike-heeled feet, then took a fifty out of his pocket. "How about a lap dance for old Uncle Bob?"

She smiled and spun carefully on her heels, waving her ass in his face. She tried to feel sexy doing it, but mostly it gave her the urge to giggle. "Sorry," she said. "I'm not doing lap dances yet. I need safety training."

"Safety training? Shit." He laughed. "I'm not dangerous, honey, you can come sit on my lap."

She turned around, knelt down, and wiggled her pussy inches from his nose. "If you come back tomorrow, I should be able to."

He licked his lips, and his feverish eyes finally wandered up to her face. Then he chuckled and shook his head slightly, wandering off to the other side stage, where a girl the DJ had introduced as Desiree was dancing. Riel got back on her feet and heaved a sigh of relief, wondering how long she could use that excuse.

The departed man was replaced by a pair of drunken younger guys, but she was distracted from her customers by Laina taking the main stage.

Laina didn't have a fancy costume on like some of the other girls. She just walked gracefully onto the platform wearing nothing but red heels. Riel could see her lean muscles moving under her pale, perfect skin. Her breasts were large and ripe-looking, her ass like a round peach, her belly perfectly flat. She didn't have any tattoos or piercings to mar that expanse of translucent flesh, but Riel noticed the shiny slash of a scar below her ribs, and wondered about it.

Then she began to dance. It wasn't exactly provocative; she didn't jiggle or gyrate. She arched and twisted, twined her limber body around the pole like a vine. She exuded the ice-queen aura that she had when Riel first laid eyes on her, but as she contorted that fabulous body, she seemed to ache with need. Riel could see all the places on that body where she wanted to put her fingers and lips and tongue, and got the impression that, with just one touch, she could cause Laina's cold exterior to melt into fire.

Riel suspected she wasn't the only one who felt that way. Men crowded around Laina's stage like hungry zombies.

Then a voice called her attention back to her own stage, and she realized she'd quit even trying to dance. One of the young guys was talking to her. "Hey, can I get a lap dance?" he asked, his unsteady eyes on her.

He smiled, his nervous, drunken cockiness lending him a sort of charm. For a moment, Riel considered taking him up on it. She wondered if she could make herself come, rubbing against him while watching Laina dance.

But then the song ended, and Laina left the stage. Riel wilted a bit. She smiled at the young guy. "Sorry," she said. "It's my first day and I need safety training. Come back tomorrow."

***

At five o'clock another girl came to take her

place, and Riel heaved a sigh of relief. *Maybe I'll get back in time for Evan,* she thought, a spark of hope trying to kindle in her breast. She wrapped herself in a robe and went back into the dressing room.

Laina was at the vanity when Riel flopped onto the couch and unstrapped her heels, rubbing her sore feet.

"How are you feeling?" Laina asked, running red lipstick over her lips. Her silken dressing gown was draped across her creamy thighs. Riel's eyes skimmed the length of her long, white legs, which were bent over the side of the chair, her bare feet curled together.

"Every part of me hurts," Riel said, forcing her gaze to the walls and arching her back to stretch it out. She pulled on her jeans.

"It gets easier," Laina said.

"I hope so," Riel muttered. She caught Laina's reflection watching her from the mirror with eyes full of pity.

"All of it gets easier," Laina said.

Riel tried to smile as she hooked her bra and pulled her sweater back on. "You're a really good dancer, by the way," she said, heat rising to her cheeks. She saw Laina's lips twitch in the mirror.

"Thanks."

"Why…why are you here, anyway? I mean, no offense, but you're too good for this place."

Laina went still. Her eyes darted to Riel's, then away again. "It's not a bad job. The money's good, and dancing is really fun."

"You know what I mean," Riel said. "You're too

64

good to be working for someone like Isaias."

Laina winced slightly, and stared at her lap. "I...Isaias did me a favor in a low point in my life. It's taking me a while to pay it back."

Riel's cheeks heated up again, with anger this time. She knew all about Isaias' "favors." She was about to risk asking her what it was when the door to the dressing room burst open.

Both of them turned, startled. Isaias stood in the doorway, looking at Riel with a strange smile.

"*Safety training?*" he said. Riel's heart clenched. "You've been telling guys you couldn't give them lap dances because you needed *safety training?*"

She and Laina exchanged a quick look, and Riel thought she saw amusement and some pride in the other woman's eyes. It gave her courage, and she sat up straight, staring him down.

"You can't make me do that, Isaias. You can make me dance, but you can't make me touch anybody."

His strange smile grew a bit wider, and Riel began to wish she'd chosen different words. Maybe she should have been a bit less defiant.

"We'll see what I can make you do, Rielita."

"I'll go over it with her tomorrow," Laina said quickly. "I'll make her comfortable. You've got to give her time, Isaias, this stuff isn't as easy as you'd think."

There was a moment when Isaias didn't say anything, and Riel's heart pounded in her throat. He let out a breath. "Okay, whatever, just...I don't want to hear any more stories about you, Riel. You've caused me enough problems as it is. Now come on, let's go home."

He turned and walked out. Riel and Laina exchanged a long look. "Thank you," Riel murmured, and she saw a flash of Laina's beautiful but perturbed smile before getting up and following Isaias out the door.

It was raining hard outside, the parking lot a mess of oily puddles and sopping trash, gloomy in the grey twilight. Riel shivered as she climbed into the passenger seat of Isaias' truck, shivering harder when he cranked the engine and the vents blasted chilly air. She pulled her arms inside her damp sweater, wrapping them around her bare torso, but it didn't help.

Isaias sat with the engine idling, not making any move to pull out of the parking lot. With creeping dread, Riel could feel him watching her, and finally forced herself to meet his gaze. His eyes were hard and mean, and she instinctively cringed away against the passenger door.

"You're so full of shit, Riel," he said.

"Isaias, I—"

He pounded the steering wheel. "How hard is it to rub up on some guy? It's not like you're virginal. Why you gotta fuck with me like this after all I've done for you?"

Riel's fear battled with her anger, and she worked at suppressing both of them, her heart hammering. Instinctively, she put her arms back through her sleeves, so she'd have the use of them. "It's not as easy as you think, like Laina said. Just give me a little while to get used to the idea."

He smiled in a way that made Riel feel like she

was falling into a dark abyss. "I could get you used to the idea," he said. "You need a lesson? I'll give you a crash course."

The heater vents were starting to warm up, but she suddenly felt much colder. He reached out and caught her wrist.

"Isaias—"

He pulled her toward him, and she tried to jerk away. He grasped her wrist tighter, pulling harder. "Come over here, Riel, I'll show you how it's done."

Riel's ears rang. Her gaze darted out the windshield, looking for a means of escape, someone to cry out to, but all she saw were dumpsters and soggy blackberry vines in the vacant lot next door. "Isaias, please…"

"The hard-to-get act is interesting, but it's time to let it go." He caught her other wrist, his fingers crawling up to her elbows, pulling her halfway out of her seat. Riel felt sick, not knowing what to do. If she fought him, he'd probably hurt her. He had before when she hadn't done what he wanted. Possibilities flashed through her mind in a panicked montage. If he left bruises on her, would it get her out of working at this place for a while?

"Come on, Riel."

He tugged hard, and she slid awkwardly into the space between the seats, on one knee. "Isaias…"

A loud buzzing broke into their struggle. They both froze, and it took Riel a moment to realize that it was Isaias' phone on the center console. The screen showed it was Mama Maria calling.

He cursed and released his grip on her, picking

up the phone and jabbing the answer button. "*Que hay*, Mama?" he barked. Riel scrambled back into her seat as Isaias launched into an argument with his mother in Spanish, something about some money someone wasn't giving them on time. For a moment she considered diving out the door and running off into the rainy twilight. But where would she go? She had no money, nobody to take her in. A dull ache filled her, and she strapped herself into the seat with her seatbelt, as if that would keep him from grabbing hold of her again if he wanted to.

Isaias finished the argument and slammed the phone back on the console, sighing and raking his fingers through his hair. Then, to Riel's immense relief, he put the truck in reverse and pulled out of the parking lot. "That fucking bitch," he muttered, but Riel had nothing but words of praise for Mama Maria right then.

He didn't try to speak to her further as they drove home, seeming lost in his thoughts. When they pulled into the driveway, she unbuckled her seatbelt and jumped out before he had even come to a full stop. She ran inside and found Lizette in the kitchen, stirring a kettle on the stove.

Her sister looked up wide-eyed when she came in. "Riel, what's wrong?"

"Nothing," she lied. "Hey, has Evan stopped by?"

Lizette's brow furrowed, and she shook her head. "No. Why?"

Riel's heart sank, but it was still early. He could still come. "If he shows up, I'll be in my room."

"Okay, Riel, but—"

Riel didn't stick around to hear what else her sister had to say. She heard the front door open as Isaias came in. "I'm going to go practice my guitar now," she said. Riel left her sister to look after her worriedly as she dodged out the kitchen door and down the hallway, locking herself in her room.

She heaved a sigh of relief. As long as she stayed in here, she should be safe. *Until Evan comes.*

She sat on her bed, picked up her guitar, and hugged it like a huge, wooden teddy bear. *Evan, please come,* she prayed. She fought back tears and started to play. The music drove everything else out of her head: Isaias, the leering men at the club, even Evan—almost.

She didn't know how long she'd been playing when there was a light knock on the door, and she looked up, her heart accelerating.

"Riel," Lizette's voice called, "*está la cena.*"

Riel's heart stumbled and fell. She looked at the clock; it was almost seven. If he hadn't come by now, he wasn't coming. "I'm not hungry," she called back, trying to keep the disappointment out of her voice.

There was a pause. "Everything okay?"

Riel wiped her eyes. She should be able to confide in her sister, but she just couldn't. Not about this. Lizette had enough to deal with without knowing the full extent of her husband's assholery, and she couldn't even bring herself to say Evan's name aloud right now. "I'm fine," she said. "Just tired."

After a moment, Lisette said, "Okay, but I'll save some for you in the fridge. It's *sopas.*"

69

The floor creaked as she walked off, and Riel resumed playing. Tears spilled over, falling onto her guitar. *I don't have anyone.* Her throat grew tight as she thought of Marissa, back in prison. Had she found another girlfriend yet? She'd probably never know. *And Evan...*

She took a constricted breath, which shook with sobs. Her fingers got tangled up on the fretboard. She gave up playing and pressed her forehead into the cool, polished wood of the instrument's body. *Stop blubbering. You'll figure a way out of this on your own. You know you can't rely on other people to save you. You have to save yourself.*

After a moment she quit crying, but she felt completely numb and worn out. She set her guitar aside, turned off the light, and curled up under the blankets, letting that horrible day slip out of her consciousness as she fell asleep.

***

The next morning, Riel didn't get up until Lizette knocked for the third time. By the time she showered and got dressed, Isaias was waiting for her in the kitchen, looking thunderous.

"Make her a sandwich or something to go," he ordered Lizette. "We've got to get moving."

Lizette nodded, and started piling fried eggs and bacon onto slices of toast. She slathered on mayo and *Tapatío* sauce before wrapping it in wax paper and handing it to Riel with a worried look. "Have a good day at work," she said quietly.

Riel didn't respond. Isaias was tapping his foot,

so she followed him out of the kitchen and through the front door.

A biting wind seemed to drive the icy rain clean through Riel's bones, but she felt like she'd rather be stuck out in the weather than climbing into the cab of the pickup with Isaias. She got in anyway, feeling so hopeless that she wondered if she had the strength to fight him off if he made more advances.

Isaias got in and started up the engine, sighing through pursed lips as he backed out. "You gonna be a good girl today?" he asked.

"Yes, Isaias." She stared at her lap, barely seeing the sandwich in her hands. It was still warm, and the aroma of it made her stomach rumble, even though she didn't feel hungry. She realized she hadn't eaten since breakfast the day before. Mechanically, she unwrapped it and took a bite.

"Today's Friday, and I want you to work late," Isaias said. "We usually get good crowds in after five. And none of this *safety training* bullshit, Riel, I'm serious. What fucking good are you if you don't do lap dances? We don't make jack shit on drinks and regular tips. All of the money is from lap dances."

And whatever else. She chewed her sandwich in silence. To Riel's relief, he turned up the radio and didn't attempt more conversation, singing off-key along with the songs, getting most of the words wrong.

Robert was behind the bar again when they got there. "Hey, Isaias, hey, Riel," he said cheerfully as they walked in. "Laina's already here, and she's waiting for you in the back, Riel."

A small bubble of happiness rose up through the heavy layer of Riel's depression. *At least if I'm stuck here, I'm stuck with Laina.*

"Thanks, Robert," she said. Ignoring Isaias' suspicious look, she left him behind and went down the hall to the dressing room.

Laina was at the vanity table, dabbing at her burgundy lipstick. One small braid fell over her left shoulder, and the rest of her hair tumbled down her back in a thick, silvery cascade. She looked around when Riel came in, and smiled. "Hey," she said.

"Good morning," Riel said. She tried to smile back, and Laina's smile faded.

"He's being a dick to you, isn't he?" she asked quietly.

Riel shrugged dully. "He's a dick, so he's going to act like one."

Laina smiled hesitantly. "Both of us are going to get away from him someday."

Riel nodded. "Someday."

"Someday soon," Laina said, and Riel could tell she was trying to sound more positive than she felt. "But for now, let's just do what we need to do to get through today." She turned her chair around and beckoned with a manicured hand. "Come on," she said.

Riel blinked, not quite allowing herself to hope, and Laina smiled the way Riel liked, her face lighting up. "I promise I'll be nice. I was just going to give you a lap dance lesson, unless it makes you uncomfortable." She snorted. "I guess we could call it safety training."

Riel smiled for real. "It doesn't make me

uncomfortable," she said too quickly, and her cheeks got hot.

"Well, come on then."

She went over shyly, and Laina took her hand. Riel's skin tingled where it touched hers.

"Sit down," Laina said, her lips quirking wryly.

She did, straddling the other dancer and lowering herself onto her lap. Riel's breath caught in her throat. Laina's beautiful breasts were pressed up against hers, and her fascinating lips were only inches away.

"Giving a lap dance isn't hard," Laina said, "but there is a sort of art to it. You want to get the guy off as quick as possible, so you can get your money and...well..." Her blue eyes filled with pity.

"So Isaias can get my money, and I can move on to the next nasty pervert," Riel said, and Laina winced.

"I'm sorry, Riel, that's such bullshit about the money."

"It's okay," Riel said, smiling faintly. "Just show me how to do this."

Laina returned the smile. "Every man is a little different. You have to maintain eye contact, watch his face to see what he likes, how he likes it...some like you to rub up against them slow, some like it fast. Some want you to giggle and bounce, some want you to purr. You get a feeling for what they want after a while, even at first glance. Then it becomes sort of like a game, like acting, and it's fun, really. At least when they smell okay." She wrinkled her nose.

Riel looked into Laina's beautiful, blue eyes,

which were the color of the sky in early spring. There was more kindness in them than there had been when they first met, but they were still distant, cold; Riel could sense the wall Laina built around her feelings, and she wanted that wall to crumble. Gently, she pressed her pussy up against Laina's, through the layers of spandex and denim. A wave of heat coursed through her, and she wondered what it would feel like if they were both naked. She pressed harder, moving her hips in slow circles. She felt herself get wet, and a mischievous grin rose to her face. "Like this?" she asked.

Laina's pupils grew larger, and she blinked. A faint, lopsided smile flitted over her lips. "Not bad."

Riel held the other woman's gaze as she moved, and Laina's breathing quickened, her lips parting slightly. Their nipples touched, and she felt them harden. Riel wanted to feel the other woman's breasts, to run her hands up under her t-shirt and squeeze them, to feel her soft skin under her palms. She remembered what they'd looked like yesterday when Laina danced, and longing took her over.

Laina took an unsteady breath. Riel gazed into those blue eyes and saw the uncertainty in them, but she could feel Laina's defenses coming down. She could see the wildfire underneath the cold exterior—Riel wanted that fire to engulf her. She leaned down, putting her lips close to the other woman's ear, slowly dragging her thumbs along the curve of Laina's waist. "I'm new at this," she whispered. "Tell me how you want it, Laina."

Riel heard Laina sigh, and she felt the other dancer's body start to move against hers. "I want it just like that," Laina said softly, the words pouring forth in a rush. Riel looked her in the eyes again, saw their blue ice burning hot.

"Oh, God, Riel, don't stop that," Laina said, her eyes fluttering closed. She arched her limber back, bringing their bodies even closer together, and Riel leaned forward and kissed her.

Her lips were soft, her tongue sweet, but Riel could feel her trembling slightly, still fighting her need, trying to put out that beautiful blaze that burned in her core. Riel put her arms around Laina. She moved her hips with slow insistence, and a small moan escaped the other woman's lips as they kissed.

Riel's fingers crept under Laina's t-shirt, caressing her smooth waist, running up lightly along her skin and feeling Laina shiver. Then her hands found her round, warm breasts, and Riel pried them from the lacy cups of her bra, gently pinching her nipples.

Laina's defenses finally broke. Her lips and tongue pressed against Riel's, burning with hot passion. She pressed the heels of her hands into Riel's ass, bringing her closer. Riel rubbed against her; she felt her need growing. Laina's hips shuddered as she gasped and moaned, and Riel rubbed harder, pleasure breaking over her sweetly as she came, feeling every curve of Laina's beautiful body writhe in the grip of her own orgasm.

Riel heard the door open behind her. She jumped, and the only thing that kept her from falling off Laina's lap was the fact that her arms were around her.

Isaias stood in the doorway, his eyes wide with surprise. Her heart hit a brick wall. She felt Laina tense up.

"Oh, I see," he said. "We've got a little something going on in here. Very interesting."

Riel stood up quickly, stumbling as she backed away from Laina's chair. She kept her eyes on Isaias, wiping the sweat from the back of her neck. "She was just training me," Riel said.

Isaias grinned wryly, his gaze seeming to swallow her up. "That's a good idea," he said. "Why don't we have a little more training, all three of us together?"

A wave of nausea washed over her, and she and Laina exchanged a darting glance.

"That's okay, Isaias, I think I'm all trained up now," Riel said.

Isaias lifted an eyebrow. He turned and quietly closed the door. Then he faced them again.

"I'm curious," he said. "Did they teach you to be a dyke in prison, Riel? And I never knew that about you, either, Laina."

Riel's hands curled into fists. "Shut up, Isaias."

He walked to where Riel stood and stared down at her, his eyes flashing dangerously. She had to keep herself from backing away.

He stroked her waist lightly. "Your bitchy attitude doesn't fool me, Riel. I know how you are. A good, hard fuck with a real cock would cure your bad mood in a second."

Riel went cold. He pulled her against him, and she could feel his hard-on.

"Yeah, I could pound the bitchy right out of

you," he said. "I'll work that wet pussy until all you can do is scream for more."

"Isaias—" Laina said.

"Don't worry, Laina," he said. "I don't plan on leaving you out. This is 'training' after all, because if you two like to get gay with each other, that's something our clients will definitely be interested in."

Riel jumped back out of his grasp. "No fucking way, Isaias. And you leave Laina alone. Stop being a dick."

He gave her a cruel grin. "Oh, not this bullshit again. This act is getting so old, Riel."

Fury consumed her until she could barely see. "I can't stand you! I'd rather die than fuck you! And I won't work in this goddamn place! I won't!"

The silence rang loud as her words died away. Riel felt sick. The look on Isaias' face made her anger turn abruptly into fear.

His hand came up so quickly she didn't even have time to duck. His fist caught the side of her head, knocking her sideways into a rack of clothing. Her cheek hit the metal bar, and she went down hard on her hip.

"Stop it, Isaias!" Laina shrieked. She jumped from her chair and grabbed his thick arm, but he flung her off, sending her reeling. She stumbled on her heels and fell on her ass, her forehead smacking against the wall.

Then Isaias turned back to Riel, who sat in a pile of stripper costumes. Lights flashed behind her eyes as the sharp pain in her head slowly subsided. Her mouth tasted like puke and every beat of her heart felt like a small explosion.

Isaias stepped toward her, his lips pulled back in a sneer. "Get up, Riel. Get your fucking cunt ass off the goddamn floor."

Riel scooted back from him, but she hit the clothes rack and couldn't get far. She sat frozen as he took another step toward her. Her eyes met Laina's, who sat against the far wall holding her head. In those blue eyes was mirrored the fury and helplessness that Riel herself felt.

Then the door came open again, and Isaias turned sharply.

It was Robert. His eyes took in the scene quickly, his face going stony and blank. "Isaias, Luis is here. He's waiting in your office."

Isaias stood frozen for a moment, then spat a curse. He glanced briefly at Riel and Laina, and then pushed past Robert, stalking out.

Robert came in and shut the door. He helped Laina up, then rushed over to Riel, bending down to look at her. "Are you guys okay?" he asked.

"I'm okay," Riel said. "Is your head okay, Laina?"

"I'm fine, it's nothing." Her face contorted in fury. "That man is a fucking *piece of shit,* Robert! He hit Riel, and pushed me down!"

"Shhhh!" Robert said, glancing anxiously at the door. He gently helped Riel to her feet. "Listen, Riel," he muttered. "Evan is waiting for you out back in his car. You've got to go quick before Isaias gets wise."

It took a couple of moments for his words to hit home. Her heart took off galloping. "Evan?" She could hardly let herself believe it. How did he even know she was here?

Robert nodded, grasping her shoulder. "Come on, you've got to get out of here quick." He tugged her toward the door, but Riel stopped him.

"Laina's coming with me," she said.

Laina and Robert exchanged a glance. "I can't, Riel," Laina said.

"You can't stay here with that monster!" Riel said.

"I've got a son at home," she said quietly. "I'll be okay. You go. I'll get my chance later."

Riel looked at Laina. Her hair was messed up, and a lump was rising on her forehead where it had hit the wall, but those blue eyes didn't show any pain or anguish. Her defenses had gone back up. Riel's throat tightened. "Laina..."

"I'll take care of her," Robert said. "I promise."

"He always has," Laina said. "I'll be okay. *Go, Riel!*"

Before Riel could say anything else, Robert put his arm around her shoulders and guided her out the door, into the hallway. There was an exit at the back end of it, and he took her through it quickly.

Outside, a blue Mustang sat in the pouring rain, its engine idling. The driver's tinted window rolled down, and her heart swelled as she saw Evan behind the wheel. His full lips curled into a smile that was almost shy, and he looked at her hopefully.

Tears sprung hot into Riel's eyes. Robert pulled her through the chill rain toward the passenger side and opened the door for her. He squeezed her shoulder as she got in. "You take care, Riel," he said. "Run far and fast, and never come back."

"Take care of Laina," she said, her voice thick.

Robert smiled. "I will."

He shut the door, and Evan hit the gas, tearing out of the parking lot and onto the road, leaving Robert to watch after them in the rain.

Chapter Six

Riel hugged herself tightly as they sat in freeway traffic, heading south. The rain pounded against the windshield, and the defroster whooshed at full-blast, keeping the windows from fogging.

Evan cursed, his jaw tight. "I'm going to fucking kill that fucker."

"It's okay, Evan."

"It's *not* okay." His eyes burned an almost radioactive green. "I had no fucking idea he was violent like that. I'm so sorry, Riel."

"It's not your fault."

"I should have dragged you out of that house during the party whether you wanted me to or not."

She snorted. "Like you could have."

He glanced at her, and his expression softened. "You're right. You would have pulled those sexy guns on me." He squeezed her biceps, and Riel giggled. She was so happy to be back with Evan. He was so sweet, so *normal*. No matter how messy life got, he made it seem like everything was okay.

He sighed, raking his fingers through his curly

hair. "I'm sorry I didn't come last night. I figured it would be easier sneaking you away from that bar than risking a fight with that dick, and maybe Mama Maria."

She leaned her head against his shoulder. "How did you even know I was there? Isaias said he scared you off."

"Isaias doesn't scare me. I figured he might pull something like that, trying to run me off, and I also figured he might try to make you work at that goddamn bar of his. I told Robert that if you showed up there, to call me. So I coordinated something with Luis this morning to make sure penis face was out of the way long enough for you to get out."

Riel felt a prickle of fear. "Robert isn't going to get in trouble with Isaias, is he? Or Laina, or this Luis guy? Won't he know they're involved?"

"No way. He doesn't even know I'm friends with Robert or Luis. That dude doesn't pay attention. Robert and Laina will just say you ran out into the rain, and that dipshit will probably sit around all day, thinking you'll crawl back as soon as you're cold and hungry enough."

"I hope you're right."

He put his arm around her shoulders and gave her a squeeze. "I am. That dude's a dipshit. Mama Maria runs everything. She might figure out that you've gone off with me, but she'll just think you had my number. She won't know Robert or anyone is involved."

Riel pressed the heels of her hands into her eyes. "But my sister and nieces…"

Evan sighed and kissed the top of her head, stroking the curve of her neck with his thumb. "You can't save the world without saving yourself first. You going back there won't help anybody."

"But—"

"We'll figure out some way to get them away from that stupid man-cunt, I promise, or at least some way to give them the option. I've talked to Lizette about it a little, and I don't even know if she'd leave. She loves him, for whatever reason."

Riel's stomach turned over dully, and she nestled into the crook of his arm, taking a deep breath. "I'll convince her. She doesn't need him, or his money. She's got to get out of there."

Traffic was at a complete standstill. Evan put the car in park and leaned back in his seat, pulling her closer. "We'll get ourselves set up nice somewhere. We'll buy a huge house down in Mexico with six bedrooms, convince all of them to come. Laina and Robert too." He gave her a boyish grin, and a sweet ache spread through Riel's breast. Did he really mean it?

His grin faltered, and he brushed her hair back from her face. "Ah, Riel, you're so beautiful. I missed that sweet smile of yours." He leaned down and kissed her, and Riel sank into the bliss of it, feeling his hot lips, his breath, and the taut muscles of his body against hers.

How could she not have seen it before? All those months they'd spent on the road together, she'd thought they had just been friends, but now she realized she'd always felt like this about him. She'd just been afraid to admit it, even to herself, because she didn't know if he felt the same way, and didn't want to get hurt.

Then a horn blasted behind them, and they broke apart. The car in front of them had moved forward. Evan cursed, put the car in gear and crept up behind it.

Riel cuddled up against him, closing her eyes. Whether or not he wanted more than a friends-with-benefits relationship, he'd still saved her. She was away from Isaias. As soon as she could, she'd get Lizette and her daughters out of there. Laina too.

And she'd make Isaias pay. She'd make that bastard *hurt* for what he'd done to her.

***

They made it all the way to Redding that night before they were too tired to go on. Evan insisted she wait in the car while he checked into a casino resort outside of town, and she watched him walk off towards the lobby, a confused scowl on her face. Riel hunched down in her seat, staring out the window at the first stars glimmering on the horizon, and wondered why, if Evan was trying to save paying an extra-person charge, he'd chosen someplace that looked so expensive.

Riel was startled out of her daydreams about living in a house with Evan and a cat when Evan opened the door for her, smiling. She climbed out into the balmy air, a soft breeze curling around her body. It was so much warmer here than in Portland.

Evan walked around to the back of the car and started pulling suitcases out. "Can you get the third one?" he asked.

For a moment, Riel thought he had found a way to bring her clothes along. But as she wheeled the suitcase towards the hotel's side entrance, she felt how heavy it was.

She arched her eyebrows at him. "I guess we're bringing a present to Mishmash," she said quietly.

His lips twitched into a dry smirk. "Maybe a little something, yeah."

Riel smacked him lightly on the arm as he held the door open for her. "Evan! You didn't think to mention that part to me?" She glanced around nervously. "And why didn't you have it in the secret compartment?"

He rubbed the spot where she'd hit him, pursing his lips theatrically. "Jeez, Riel, you gotta watch you don't beat me up, now that you've been working out."

She stood, glaring at him, and his expression softened and became sheepish. He jerked his chin toward the open door. "We'll discuss it in our room."

"Fine."

As they strode down the hall, his phone dinged in his back pocket, and he pulled it out, grinning as his eyes skimmed over the screen. "Robert says Isaias still hasn't figured out you're not coming back. He and Laina are fine, everything is cool."

Riel let out a breath she hadn't been aware she was holding. "Good."

She followed him to the elevator in silence. She wasn't really angry with him about the drugs, but the sudden realization that they were hauling contraband had hit her like a bad bout of flu. Cold sweat prickled the back of her neck and her stomach seemed to fill with rocks. Before she'd been busted, there had been a sort of excitement to running— pride that she was getting away with something illegal and dangerous. But prison had changed that. More than anything, she didn't want to go back to that place. Riel swallowed hard and tried to grapple her fluttering heart back into a normal rhythm.

They took the elevator to the very top floor. Evan swiped the key card at the door to their room and held it open for her.

As she wheeled the suitcase in, she paused. This was no normal hotel room—it was a suite. It had a sitting room with a leather sofa and chairs. On the coffee table was a gigantic bouquet of roses and a gift basket full of what looked like chocolate, wine, and bubble bath. "Evan…"

He smiled tentatively. "I figured you could use something a little special after what you've been through, so I got a package deal. Comes with a nice dinner too."

She dropped the suitcase and fell into his arms. He held her close, stroking her back with gentle hands. She looked up at him and had to blink back tears. "Evan, thank you."

He grinned teasingly, wiping an escaped tear from her cheek. "Jeez, Riel, it's just some flowers and junk."

"You went through all that trouble to save me, and then you do something so nice." She wanted to ask him why, but the words wouldn't come.

His smile faded. He stroked her cheek with his

thumb, brushing away another tear. "Worth it a million times over," he said.

She stood on her tiptoes and kissed him, feeling his gorgeous lips against hers. How could she have ever taken them for granted? The last few days had been difficult. She'd thought he'd run off and abandoned her, that she'd never see him again...

Riel pulled him down onto the floor, pushed him onto his back, and straddled him. She grinned. He smiled back, running his hands up to her shoulders, pulling her closer. "I'm glad you're safe," he said. "I'm glad you came with me."

Her heart skipped a beat. "Me too." She leaned down and kissed him, and felt him getting hard under his jeans. Her eyes fluttered closed. She slid her pussy along the length of his cock, slowly, then rubbed faster, aching for it. He grabbed her ass and squeezed it, and she pressed harder against him. She could feel his breath coming quicker, the urgency in his kiss and his touch. He tugged at the waistband of her jeans, and pressed his lips against her ear. "These clothes are really starting to annoy me."

She grinned and pulled off her shirt, then her jeans, tossing them over in a heap by the forgotten suitcases. He lay staring at her, his eyes glazing over. "You have no idea how beautiful you are." He ran his fingers along her bare hips, up her belly, and unhooked the front clasp of her bra. Riel let it slide off her arms, flinging it aside. A faint smile touched his lips as he cupped her breasts. "You're the most beautiful girl."

Her entire body filled with warmth, and she smiled teasingly in an attempt to cover up her blush.

"Speaking of clothes being annoying, you're pretty hot with them on, but even better with them off."

He ignored her, grasping her waist and pulling her gently toward him, bringing his mouth to her breasts, circling her nipples with his tongue. She gasped, then moaned when he pulled the crotch of her panties aside with his other hand, sliding two fingers inside her. She pressed against them, feeling them go deeper. He slid them in and out, sucking on her nipples, and she placed her palm on his chest, gently forcing him away. "You're going to make me come already," she said breathlessly. "I want you inside me." She kissed him lightly. "It feels so good with you inside me."

He made a low noise in his throat. She lifted his shirt up, pressing her lips against his taut belly just above his navel, feeling him shiver. He pulled his shirt off as she unbuttoned his jeans and pulled them down. He kicked them off and she tugged off his boxers and tossed them aside. Soon after, she quickly pulled off her panties. He reached out to pull her on top of him, but she resisted, and instead brought her lips to the head of his long cock.

He cried out as she took it in her mouth. "Riel…" She slid her lips and tongue along his shaft as far as she could, caressing his balls with gentle fingers. "Oh, God," he gasped, and desperately pulled her away and toward him, kissing her on her lips. She straddled him and slid his cock inside her slowly, a moan rising up out of her throat. She felt his lips tense slightly under hers. Riel could feel him trembling, and she knew he was trying hard to not lose control.

She made her hips stay still, though she desperately wanted the pleasure of Evan rubbing against all the places inside her. She kissed him gently, and he took a long, shuddering breath. "Oh, Riel." He gasped.

She began to move in slow circles, his cock moving inside her, feeling the ache in her grow. He slid his hands down her waist and grasped her hips, arching toward her and thrusting himself inside. She sat up on her knees, moving faster, bringing him deeper, and he moved with her, squeezing the firm cheeks of her ass and circling her nipples with his tongue. She closed her eyes and rode faster and harder until the heat burst inside her. Her lips parted in a wordless cry as wave after wave of pleasure broke over her, and he gasped her name over and over, thrusting himself inside her as he finally let himself go.

She collapsed on top of him, panting, and he held her, running his fingers lightly along her spine as he took a contented breath. "Riel, you're so amazing," he said.

She stretched alongside him on the floor. "*You're* amazing."

He rolled over and took her in his arms, frowning slightly. "I'm sorry about the drugs, and about not telling you right away. Mishmash just needed a shipment brought down, and I thought it was a good opportunity to kill two birds with one stone, make a little cash." He rubbed his nose. "Well, a lot of cash, really. That's why the suitcases weren't in the secret compartment. I have more in there. It was a bigger than normal shipment this time."

Riel's scalp prickled, but she shrugged. "It's okay. I knew we were going to be doing that. But running drugs south seems weird…"

"Not all drugs come across the border from Mexico, you know," he said, pinching her nose. "This came by boat. Mishmash has a pretty good system going."

"I guess I never thought that much about how it works. I don't really want to know."

He brushed his lips across hers. "I know. You want to get out of this business. And we will." He gazed at her. "I'm glad you came with me, even though it's not really, you know, what you want to be doing. It was…it was hell yesterday, knowing you were working at that place." He winced. "I wanted to go get you right away, but Robert told me it was too dangerous, that Isaias had his eye on you."

"It's okay," Riel said. "It turned out okay in the end." She snuggled closer into his arms, burning the skin of her hips slightly on the rough carpet.

His lips pressed tightly together. "It didn't really turn out okay, though. That fucker hurt you." His fingers came up to gently caress the lump on her head where Isaias' fist had caught her.

"It barely hurts," she said.

"And just the thought of you, all those perverted men groping you like you're some sex doll." His jaw clenched, and Riel's heart beat faster. Was he jealous?

"I didn't touch any men," she said. "I told all the ones that wanted lap dances that I couldn't yet,

90

because I needed lap dance safety training."

His jaw loosened slightly, and his lips twitched. "Are you serious?"

She grinned. "I can't believe it worked."

He laughed, his hands caressing her naked body. "Safety training. I can just see you practicing on one of those crash-test dummies."

"With some government inspector making notes on a clipboard."

Both of them convulsed in giggles. Soon, Evan's face became still and serious. He pushed a lock of messy hair back from her cheek. "You really didn't have to give any lap dances?"

She bit her lip, her eyes darting away from his. His caressing hands went suddenly still. "What? What's wrong?"

She looked up at him. Part of her wished she was a better liar so she could just avoid this subject. But another part wanted to see how he'd react, if he'd get jealous or angry. "I did give one," she said.

His lips drew tight again, and she watched him closely.

"To Laina," she said.

He blinked. His brow furrowed slightly. "You gave Laina a lap dance?"

Riel nodded. "It was training. Isaias got super pissed that I was giving the safety training excuse, so Laina just wanted to help make me comfortable."

His hands began to move again, distractedly feeling her curves. A lopsided smile flitted across his lips. "But wait…did you like…was it a real lap dance?"

Riel's cheeks burned. She was barely able to

meet his gaze, and his eyebrows shot up. "Whoa," he said, squirming slightly. "No offense, Riel, but that's...that's sorta...neat. Did you, like, you know..." He trailed off, looking flustered, and Riel grinned cheekily.

"I got off," she said, "and so did she."

Evan stared at her, wide-eyed. "So you, do you, you know...like girls that way?"

She gazed up at him defiantly. "Yes. I had a girlfriend in prison, named Marissa." Her heart squeezed, and she swallowed hard.

He frowned, his eyes distant. She waited tensely. She liked him, she liked him a lot, but she wouldn't be judged by him. "Does that bug you?" she finally asked, not able to keep the anger out of her voice.

He blinked, seeming to come back to himself. "No. I mean...it's a lot easier to think about you with other women than with other dudes, no offense. A lot easier."

She relaxed slightly. "No offense taken."

"But you do like men too, right?"

She grinned at him in disbelief, but it faded as she saw the sincerity of his insecurity. "I just fucked your brains out, and you ask me if I like men?"

"Well, you could be fantasizing about me being someone else," he said.

She shook her head. "I like fucking you, Evan. I...I like you. I've never liked another man, but..." She couldn't finish the sentence. She looked shyly up into his eyes.

"You've never liked another man? Seriously?"

"No. I've never been with a man besides you. I haven't been with *anyone* besides you and

Marissa…and that lap dance I gave Laina."

He smiled lopsidedly and pressed his lips against her neck. She could feel his cock growing hard again. Then he kissed her, his fingers creeping down to gently rub her slippery clit, and she forced back her worries about how many other girls *he* had been with. He was older, and really good-looking, and she probably didn't want to know. Instead, she just gave herself up to the pleasure of his touch.

Chapter Seven

It was growing dark the next day when they pulled into their hotel in downtown San Diego. The hotel building rose up sleek and gleaming into the twilight sky. The shoreline spread out behind it, palm trees silhouetted against the last orange-green light on the horizon.

"Jeez, Evan, you're not skimping on the hotels," she said.

He shut off the car and leaned over to kiss her, his hand working its way under her shirt to squeeze one of her tits. "It's not too expensive," he muttered. "Besides, I liked fucking you in that spa tub last night. I was hoping we could try it again."

She snorted, but part of her couldn't help but worry that if he was flinging money around like this, he wasn't really thinking about saving up for the long-term. *All that stuff about quitting running, getting a house, helping me go to college, it was just talk. If I want out of this life, I'm going to have to do it myself.*

He pulled his lips from hers and looked at her

worriedly. "You all right?"

She made herself smile. "I'm fine. Just hungry and tired of being in the car."

He kissed her on the forehead. "Well, let's go check in and get some food before we call Mishmash."

Riel winced. She wasn't looking forward to seeing him. She was Isaias' sister-in-law, after all. How suspicious would he be of her?

They unloaded the suitcases and rolled them into the lobby, and Riel tried not to think about how much prison time she was lugging behind her. What if Isaias figured out what was going on, and snitched them off as revenge? She wiped the sweat from the back of her neck and pushed the thought away. There was nothing she could do about it right now.

A statuesque blonde clerk made eyes at Evan as they walked up to the reception desk.

"Checking in?" she asked with a smile that made Riel's guts twist.

She's flirting with him right in front of me. She didn't blame the lady for thinking she had a chance. The clerk was almost six feet tall and put together like some sort of Danish supermodel, and Riel stood there, just over five feet tall and in the same clothes as yesterday, for lack of other options. But then Evan put an arm around her, pulling her close, and Riel gazed up at the other woman a bit smugly.

"Reservation for Theodore Anderson," he said, tugging his wallet out and sliding a credit card over the marble-topped counter.

The woman checked them in and handed over

their key cards. Riel glanced sidelong at him as they headed for the elevators. "I didn't know you had a false identity," she murmured.

"Of course. I don't want Mama Maria to find us. Mishmash should have documents for you too, when he comes."

The elevator came, and they got in. "Really? Already?"

He smiled and pinched her nose. "I have to admit I was really hoping you'd come with me, so I paid for them before you were even out of prison. I figured, even if I couldn't convince you to come, it was worth the expense, just in case."

The doors opened again and they got out on their floor. Tinted windows lined the corridor, and Riel gazed out at the city lights far below. "Jeez, Evan," she murmured. "Isaias must have paid you way more than he paid me. Fake identities aren't cheap."

Evan let out a mirthless bark of laughter as he unlocked the door to their room. "Isaias didn't really pay you, Riel. He just blackmailed you into working for him. Besides, I've always had something going on the side." He shut the door and pulled her into his arms. "Don't be nervous, Rielita. Isaias won't be able to find you now. You're safe."

She laid her ear on his chest, listening to his heartbeat. *I won't really be safe until I'm out of this business.*

***

After dinner, Evan called Mishmash and told him they'd arrived. Riel's ahi-filled stomach suddenly felt sick, and she curled up on the mattress to wait.

Evan stretched out next to her and turned on the TV. "Ooh, *Seinfeld* reruns," he said, and leaned over to kiss her neck. She knew he was trying to keep her mind off things, but that was impossible right now.

After about forty-five minutes, there was a knock on the door. Riel sat up, clutching the blankets, and Evan tousled her hair. "It's going to be all right, Rielita."

"I know," she muttered.

Evan went to answer the door, and Riel heard Mishmash's voice. "Hey, how's it going?"

"Good, good, how are you doing?" Evan said.

They came into the room, and Mismash grinned at Riel in a friendly, almost childlike way. He came over to shake her hand. "Hey, I remember you," he said. "Hard to forget a face like that."

Riel smiled. His hand was warm and dry, which made her realize she was sweating. The sleeves of Mishmash's plaid shirt were rolled up over his thick forearms, and she saw he had a bible verse tattooed on the inside of his right one.

No se angustien por el mañana, el cual tendrá sus propios afanes.

She took a deep breath, let it out. *"To each day its own problems." That's a good philosophy in this business.* "It's good to see you, Mishmash," she said.

Evan stretched back out next to her on the bed,

and Mishmash settled in a chair, tugging at the legs of his jeans so they fell straight. He was still watching her, and he grinned again, then reached into an inside pocket of his shirt and pulled out a folded manila envelope, holding it out to her. "So I hear you're starting a new life."

Riel tried to keep her hand from shaking as she took the envelope. She clutched it tightly, feeling the passport and her other fake documents within. *My new life,* she thought a bit bitterly. "Yeah," she said. "I'm done working for that dick Isaias."

He laughed. It was almost a giggle, and the sound of it made Riel smile. She had to remind herself that this guy wasn't as sweet as he seemed; he'd likely killed more than a few people. "I don't blame you," he said. "Not after what he did. I couldn't believe he'd screw over his own sister-in-law like that."

Riel glanced at Evan, her brow furrowed, wondering if he'd told him about the strip club and how Isaias had hit her. She couldn't imagine the two of them gossiping like that. But Evan looked just as confused as she did, staring at Mishmash with a frown. "What do you mean?" he asked.

Mishmash's eyebrows shot up, and his meaty lips formed an "O". Then he laughed again, slapping his stocky thighs. "Oh shit, he didn't even tell you, did he? *Chingada madre.* What a fucking *cabrón.*"

Riel's chest tightened. "What did he do?"

Mishmash gave her a hesitant look, rubbing his knuckles against his upper lip, then shrugged. "He got into a tight spot with some feds. They needed a sacrifice, I guess, because they were getting questions from higher-ups and were worried their cover would be blown. So he threw you under the bus. I heard he cut a deal in regard to your sentencing, but still, that's pretty messed up. He could have given them someone outside the family."

Riel's ears rang, and the world seemed to go dark. For a moment she thought she was going to puke and had to close her eyes. As she took deep breaths, she felt Evan's arm go around her, steadying her.

"I'm gonna kill that dick," Evan muttered. "I thought she got busted somehow fair and square, and that he just stepped in to keep her going away for hard time."

"Sorry to have to be the bearer of that bad news," Mishmash said. "I thought he at least would have told you, given you some compensation or something."

"Nope," Riel said through gritted teeth.

Mishmash's broad brow creased slightly, his shrewd eyes not leaving her face. "If that's not the reason you took off on him, then why did you?"

Riel gathered herself up. "Because he's an *asshole*, that's why. He treated me like shit. He didn't pay me. He made me do things..." She squeezed her eyes shut, catching her breath, and Evan's arm tightened around her.

"That fucker hit her," Evan said. "I don't even want to know what else he would have done to her if I hadn't gotten her out of there."

"Oh, shit, I get it," Mishmash said quietly.

"Sorry to bring it up." He chuckled darkly. "*Que putaso.* Well, you're well rid of a piece of garbage like that. Hitting females is just wrong. You don't do that."

Riel nodded, wiping her eyes. Mishmash smiled and leaned forward, patting her foot. "That crap is all over for you. You're safe with me. And maybe you'll get your chance to get back at that *culito* for what he did, eh?" He grinned wider, and Riel gazed at him, startled. Then she felt a smile spread across her face.

"Maybe," she said.

Mishmash laughed. "That's the spirit. I think we're going to enjoy working together, you and I."

A desire for revenge flared up inside Riel. All those months in prison had been because of Isaias. And then he had the audacity to try to make her pay him back for the drugs and lawyer fees.

I'll kick that guy where it hurts. I'll twist his balls into a knot. I'll make him wish he were dead and that he never heard the name Gabriella Hernandez.

Chapter Eight

They spent a few days in San Diego before heading over the border for their next pickup. Most of their days were spent at the beach, or in the Jacuzzi tub in their hotel room, though they did find time to go clothes shopping. Evan insisted on paying for everything himself; he even wanted to get her a couple of nice dresses.

"Save your money," he said. "It's your college fund."

Riel ran the fabric of the dress she was looking at between her fingers. Evan had given her half of the money he'd gotten from Mishmash for the run, and they'd set her up a bank account in her fake name— Nora Mejia. She hadn't picked it, but it had a nice sound. Mishmash would do a direct transfer for future work under the name of one of his San Diego businesses, as if she was a legitimate employee. Having the money already laundered was one of the benefits of working for him, but this perk did little to dispel her nervousness about the job in general.

"It'll take a long time to save up for college," she

101

muttered, putting the dress back on the rack. "College is expensive."

He grabbed the dress back off the rack, handing it to her again. "At least try it on. And I'll help with college and your expenses. Plus, you can get scholarships. You're smart." He ruffled her hair, grinning, then patted her ass, nudging her towards the dressing room. "Come on, Riel. Just try it on. I want to see it on you."

She rolled her eyes and ducked behind the curtain, wondering if he was really serious about helping her. *I'll believe it when I see it.*

And he had an even sweeter surprise for her after that. After they left the clothing boutique, swinging their shopping bags by their hemp handles, he took her by the hand. "Come on. I saw another store down here that I wanted to visit."

"I already have enough clothes, Evan."

He smiled, his eyes shining. "Just come on."

He led her down a side street, and Riel's breath caught when they stopped at a storefront and went in.

Guitars of all types hung from hooks on the walls. "Evan…"

"You had to leave your axe behind, and that's my fault. I know how much you miss it."

Despite her protests, he had the clerk bring her an assortment of acoustic guitars. She picked up each one, plucking out chords and listening to them resonate warmly through their hollow wooden bodies.

She stroked the polished sides of a blonde-wood classical guitar that made her bones ache with its perfect tone. It was over a thousand dollars. "This one is beautiful, but…"

"We'll take it," Evan said.

"Evan…"

He handed the clerk his credit card. "Don't listen to anything she says. We're taking this one, and a nice hard-shell case too." He kissed her lightly on the lips. "I love listening to you play. You're really good. So think of it as a present for me too."

Riel looked up at him, blinking back tears. He seemed too good to be true, and she figured there would be a catch sooner or later.

***

They checked out of the hotel early on Wednesday morning and drove over to pick up the cash for the shipment from Mishmash.

"You need to come back across the border between seven tonight and two in the morning," he said. "Use lane three when you cross. That's my guy working then, goes by the name Matt. You'll recognize him because he looks like one of those, what do you call them, elephant seals. His whole body jiggles like a fucking water balloon when he walks." He walked around doing a little belly dance to demonstrate, and they laughed.

Evan put the cash in the secret compartment of his Mustang, which was under a hidden panel in the trunk. Then they were on their way south, weaving through the early morning traffic toward the border crossing.

Riel leaned back in her seat, gazing out at the

shell-pink eastern horizon, the bronze of first sunlight creeping over the tops of the hills. Evan glanced over at her, then plugged his phone into the jack and scrolled through his music until he found what he was looking for. "I like to play a game with this band," he said. "It's called 'Try to Guess What the Fuck They're Saying.'" He tapped the screen and the music started. "Come on, grab on and go up our shirts," he sang. "The monkey tails of plastic fists."

Riel doubled up with giggles and reached out to take his hand.

"Come on, whack on, give us music squirts," he continued. "Live three times with junkie tits."

Riel laughed again, but then her smile faded, and she gazed out the window at the distant hills. "Evan," she said, "what do you think Mishmash meant about having a chance to get back at Isaias?"

He hummed along with the song, frowning. "I'm not *exactly* sure, but I get the feeling he wants to take Isaias and Mama Maria down. I think there's some territory of his that Mishmash wants to take over."

"But they work for the same boss, right? Mishmash and Isaias?"

"Ultimately, but each one of them has their own little cell, their little group of runners and other underlings. It's how the Big Boss keeps anyone from knowing too much. Each cell has its own boss and runs fairly independently, and each one knows just enough to handle their own territory. But the littler guys are always jockeying for position and power. The Big Boss doesn't care, as long as it doesn't disturb the operation. In fact, he'll reward the little bosses if they can make the operation run more smoothly by fucking over some other guy."

"Oh," Riel said. "Then that's why he wanted us to work for him. Because he wanted inside info on how Isaias' operation works."

"Exactly. He sounded me out the first time that a shipment went through his territory and up to Isaias', something that happens sometimes."

Riel pondered that. "But how do I fit in? I don't know anything."

Evan grinned. "You're Mishmash's crown jewel. His rival's sister-in-law. And you're on his side. He was very interested when I told him you were pissed off at Isaias. Plus, it's always good to have a super-hot chick running for you. No one ever suspects them."

"Unless they get turned in," she muttered.

Evan's grin disappeared. "Isaias is a fucking dick. I had no idea he did that, but it makes sense. You wouldn't have gotten busted otherwise. You're too careful."

They exchanged a glance. "And so now Mishmash wants me to help him take Isaias down."

Evan was silent for a moment, gazing out at the horizon, now flooded with sunlight. "You don't have to. We can figure out some way to get you out before you become involved in that."

"No," Riel said. "I want to. I want to make him pay."

Evan grimaced. "It's *dangerous* to get involved in that shit."

"I'm already involved. Isaias and Mama Maria

are going to figure out where we've gone sooner or later."

"Maybe not. We've got fake IDs."

"Whatever Mishmash has planned, I'm sure it'll get us noticed."

Evan shifted in his seat, rubbing the stubble on his upper lip. "Maybe."

"And whatever he has planned, I want to help. I want to take Isaias down."

Evan glanced between her and the road. Finally, he nodded. "I have your back, whatever you want to do."

Riel smiled. She leaned her head against his shoulder, and he put his arm around her.

***

The line at the border wasn't very long, and they got through without problems. Before Riel knew it, they were in Tijuana. She looked around. Everything looked pretty much the same as it had in the States, except the road signs were in Spanish. "You know what? I've never even been to Mexico," she said.

Evan laughed. "Are you kidding? Weren't your parents Mexican?"

"Yeah. I guess I have family down somewhere in Michoacán, but I've never met them. I sorta lost contact after my parents died." She stared out the window, and Evan reached over and squeezed her hand.

"I don't want to make you sad, I'm sorry. I shouldn't have brought it up."

106

"No, don't worry about it. I just sometimes wonder what would have happened if they hadn't died, if they hadn't been deported. Or, you know, if they'd actually been born in the U.S."

"I think we all wonder things like that. I mean, my parents were both born in Eureka, but I wonder what it would have been like if they weren't born dipshits."

Riel laughed, then squinted at him. "You've never really told me about your parents."

Evan shrugged. "Not much worth telling. My dad worked in the logging industry when he was younger, but he lost that job when people suddenly realized that cutting down all the trees and replacing them with Wal-Marts wasn't a sustainable practice. He was really fucking pissed about it too." Evan screwed his face up in a grimace, making his voice gruff. "If I could crush every spotted-goddamn-fucking-owl with my bare hands, I would." Riel laughed. "He ended up getting a job for some security company," Evan continued. "He worked there most of my childhood, but he started taking meth because they had him working graveyard and he said he needed it to keep his energy up. By the time I left home when I was 14, he was into it pretty bad. Lost his job not long after that. I don't even want to know what he's doing now."

Riel gazed at him, a crease in her brow. "What about your mom?"

"She worked as a supermarket checkout clerk, long hours, not much pay, plus she had me and my three sisters to take care of. Dad wasn't that nice to her, and didn't help her much. She ended up getting into meth also. Sometimes she calls me for bail money if Angela can't scrape it up."

"Angela is one of your sisters?"

"Yeah, the one who has it sorta together. Kara and Lindsey are both in and out of jail too."

"I'm sorry," Riel said, but Evan just shrugged.

"We all've got shit to deal with, right? Life's never perfect. We just do the best we can. Our upbringings could have been better, but we're doing okay, Rielita. It may not be the best right now, but we're going to keep up the struggle and we're gonna make it, right?"

"Right," she said. They grinned at each other.

"And speaking of keeping up the struggle..." They stopped at a stoplight, and he felt around under the seat, coming up with a pair of little Sig Sauer handguns. He gave one to her, and stuck the other in the waistband of his jeans. Riel stashed the gun over her hip, between her skirt and her skin, pulling her loose blouse over to hide it. It had been more than a year since she'd carried a gun, but the feeling of it against her skin was still familiar.

They met their guy on the outskirts of Tijuana, a neighborhood with little, rectangular houses packed into patches of bare dirt. Riel started to sweat as soon as she got out of the car, the sun pounding down on her. The air smelled like garbage and wood smoke, and the sound of televisions and blaring radios drifted out of the open windows of the houses.

The back of her neck prickled; it had been too long since she'd done this, and she was paranoid. She glanced around, spotting a couple kids playing in a yard and some old men sitting on a porch a couple of houses down. They were glancing at her, but they didn't look suspicious. Riel took a deep breath and checked the position of the pistol in her waistband.

A man came out of the house as they walked up, young and skinny and clean-shaven. A mottle-coated pit bull trotted at his heels.

"Hey, Theodore," he said, shaking Evan's hand. "How's it going?" Then he turned to Riel, grinning wide. "You going to introduce me to this one, Theodore?"

"Luis, this is Nora," he said.

"*Mucho gusto,*" Luis said, taking her hand.

"*Mucho gusto,*" Riel responded.

"She's my girlfriend," Evan added when Luis didn't relinquish her hand.

This information didn't seem to faze Luis, who just grinned wider, though it came as a bit of a surprise to Riel. She raised her eyebrows at Evan, but he didn't notice. His eyes were on Luis, who finally dropped her hand.

"Come on inside," he said.

They went into the house, which was dim and slightly cooler, with a fan going in one of the windows and another oscillating in the corner. An old woman sat in the tiny living room, rocking slowly in a rocking chair and watching a *telenovela*. She nodded at them as they came in, smiling vaguely. "*Buenas,*" she muttered.

"*Buenas tardes,*" Riel said. She felt the woman's curious eyes on her as they went into the tiny kitchen. Women were somewhat rare in this

109

business.

"*Sientense,*" Luis said, waving toward the chairs around the kitchen table.

They sat, and Luis disappeared into the back of the house. She and Evan exchanged a glance, and both of them wiped the sweat from the backs of their necks at the same time. Evan giggled. "It's goddamn hot in here," he said.

Riel waved away the flies trying to settle on her sticky brow. "When we retire, let's do it somewhere with air conditioning."

"Done and done," Evan said.

Luis returned, lugging a large cardboard box. He sat it on the floor, then disappeared into the back again.

Evan got up and went over to the box and started unpacking it. Inside were square packages wrapped in white plastic and stamped with a grinning emoji with heart eyes. Luis came out with another box, setting it beside the first.

Evan counted the bricks. He carefully tore aside a corner of the plastic on one of them at random, stuck his thumb in and brought it to his nostril, snorting up the white powder.

He straightened, sniffing and rubbing his nose. Luis watched him. Evan's eyebrows crept up his forehead. "Whoa," he said.

Luis laughed. "It's good, right? Got a new guy this time. Old one, he was fucking with us or something. Stuff wasn't so good anymore."

Riel's stomach clenched. She didn't want to know what had happened to the old guy.

They hauled the boxes out to the car and opened

the secret compartment. Evan handed Luis the bag of money, and then started packing bricks into the compartment while Luis leaned against the car, counting the cash.

Riel glanced around, her heart pounding in her ears. The old men were still deep in conversation on their porch, the kids still playing across the street. A pair of older ladies were strolling down the road, dressed in linen skirt suits, and Riel wondered how they didn't faint in the heat. None of them seemed to be showing any interest in what was going on here. She supposed they all knew better than to pay too much attention.

When the goods were all squared away, the compartment and the trunk lid closed, Riel felt her anxiety lessen somewhat. *Now it's just a matter of running it north.* And since Mishmash had a guy at the border, that should be easy.

Luis shook both their hands, lingering again with Riel and giving her a cocky smile. "See you again soon," he said.

"*Hasta luego, entonces,*" Riel said, heat rising to her cheeks. She could feel Evan's eyes on the two of them.

They climbed back into the car as Luis strutted back into his house, the panting pit bull trotting behind him.

Evan started the engine and cranked the air conditioning. As they bumped down the rutted, dirt road out of the neighborhood, Evan sighed and reached over to rub Riel's shoulders. "You doing okay?"

"I'm fine." She adjusted the pistol, which was

pinching her hip.

He put his arm around her and pulled her against him. "Let's go to the beach and get some seafood. We've got some time to kill before Mishmash's guy goes on duty."

"Okay." She was silent for a moment, tugging at her hair. "Evan?"

"Yeah?"

She looked up at him through her eyelashes. "Am I really your girlfriend?"

He looked sheepish, then shot her a nervous grin. "I...well...I mean, is that okay with you?" Riel's response got stuck in her throat for a moment, and Evan shifted uncomfortably. "I'm sorry, Riel, I just...I didn't like Luis looking at you like that. It just popped out. But if you'd rather it not be…"

"No," she said. "I want to be your girlfriend."

He blinked at her, then grinned.

"It just took me by surprise, that's all," Riel said. "I thought you just wanted a, you know, friends-with-benefits sort of thing."

"Sure, but friends with *exclusive* benefits."

A smile spread across Riel's face. In the middle of all this bullshit with Isaias and Mishmash, it was good to have something to be happy about. It might not work out with Evan; he may renege on his promises to help her get out of this business, get into school…he may not really have her back in regard to bringing Isaias down, but at least in this moment, she had him. *To each day, its own problems.* She scooted closer, kissing his neck. "Evan, you're sexy," she muttered.

He took one of his hands off the wheel, running

it down her back, pulling her closer. "You're going to make me crash, beautiful girl, but that's okay with me."

She laughed and pulled away slightly. "Maybe not the best idea, with what we're carrying in back."

"I think it'd still be worth it."

He pulled off on a side street and parked in an alley behind a bodega, between two dumpsters. He stashed his gun beneath the seat, then gently pulled hers loose, putting it away next to his.

He climbed between the seats into the back, pulling her with him. She climbed awkwardly over the console and into his lap, kneeling on the leather bench seat, her skirt pulling up around her hips.

He kissed her, his hands working their way down to her ass, squeezing it. "Why don't you show me what you learned about lap dances?" he said.

Riel grinned. She could feel his cock getting hard under his jeans, beneath the thin cotton of her panties. She pressed against it, rubbing up and down his long shaft, starting to get wet. She wanted to kiss him, to feel his lips against hers, and to run her fingers all over his muscled body. But she didn't; this was a lap dance.

"You're so hot," he said and reached up to fondle her breasts.

"Uh-uh," she chided. "No touching the dancers." She gently pried his hands away, placing them on the seat cushions. Riel slowly moved her hips back and forth, rubbing her clit on his throbbing cock. "You like that?" she breathed. "You like my pussy on you?"

"Oh, I like it." He arched his back slightly,

moving against her. Her hard nipples brushed against his chest, sending thrills through her. His hands crept up, grabbing her ass, but she pulled them away again, though her skin craved his touch.

"You know the rules," she said. She moved her hips faster, wanting him, her need growing, and Evan gasped and dug his fingers into the leather upholstery. His cock throbbed, and she slid her clit along the entire length of it, aching inside, her panties slippery and sopping now.

"Do you want to touch me?" she said.

"Yes, Riel…"

A bead of sweat dribbled down the back of her neck, but she barely noticed. "Do you want to stick it in me? Do you want to slide your cock inside and fuck me?"

"Oh, God, yes." His hands slid up her legs, grasping her thighs, and she wanted them there, but she pulled them slowly away again. His chest heaved, and he moaned as she rubbed faster against him. "Oh, Riel, I want you so bad. I want in that sweet pussy."

She leaned forward and gave him a light kiss, then pulled away, though it was torture. "That's against the rules."

He pressed up against her, breathing hard. Her big tits were mashed against his chest.

"Please," he begged.

"Do you want me to get fired?"

"Yes," he said. His insistent hands crept up to her tits again, squeezing them, his thumbs brushing over her nipples, and finally she couldn't take it anymore. She fumbled at the fly of his jeans, unbuttoning them, and Evan pushed them down his hips with a quick jerk. Then Riel pulled aside the soaked crotch of her panties and, as slowly as she could manage, she slid him all the way inside.

She moaned, and he sighed as he thrust himself up hard inside her, making her cry out again. "Riel," he muttered. "Riel." He thrust harder, his frantic hands working their way under her shirt, unhooking her bra, caressing her breasts. She let him pound her, feeling the ache build with each stroke. He brought his hungry lips to hers, their hot breaths mingling as he pounded deeper, squeezing her ass and pulling her against him.

"Ah, Evan," she moaned. "You're making me come. Fuck me. Hard. Hard."

With a strangled noise, he grabbed her hips and pulled her down as he thrust himself even deeper, crying out each time, her shoulder blades bouncing against the back of the driver's seat. The head of his huge, thick cock stroked her sweet spot. Her wet clit rubbed against him; pleasure took her fully. She cried out, and he let out a breath as he came hot inside her.

They sat, gasping for a moment, and Riel realized she was completely soaked in sweat. They were parked in the shade of the building, but the car was suffocatingly hot. She looked at him, and they both grinned. He wiped his forehead. "I'll leave the AC on next time," he said.

Chapter Nine

When they joined the line of cars heading north through the border, the horizon still glowed orange with the setting sun. Riel was full of food and a little bit sleepy, but couldn't stop the little jolts of nervousness creeping up her spine. Evan tapped his fingers on the doorframe, faster than the beat of the music, which played low on the stereo.

"You're nervous too, aren't you?" she asked.

He grimaced. "I guess I am. Must be because I haven't done this run before. I trust Mishmash more than I trust Isaias and Mama Maria, though. Guy's got his shit together." He passed his hand over his face. "We've got nothing to worry about."

The line of cars moved slowly, each one stopping at the border gate, their taillights glowing brighter as dusk fell. They were the third car in line, then the second, and Riel squinted through the window of the guard booth as they got closer.

Her heart jumped painfully. "Uh, Evan? We're in lane three, right?"

He glanced at her nervously. "Yeah. Why?"

116

"That guy in there doesn't look like an elephant seal."

He followed her gaze to the thin man in the guard booth, and his jaw tightened. "That can't be the right guy."

They exchanged a panicked look, Riel feeling suddenly cold. "What happened?" she asked.

"I don't know." He pulled out his phone, checking it. "Mishmash didn't call us or anything. He would have if the guy had called in sick or whatever." He threw the phone down in his lap and raked his fingers through his curls. "I don't know what happened, but let's stay cool. We're just tourists, coming back from a day at the beach. They have no reason to suspect us, even if this isn't Mishmash's guy."

Riel tried to bring her heartbeat and breathing under control. The car in front of them pulled forward, driving free onto U.S. soil, and Riel watched it depart with desperate longing, wishing they were the ones inside that car. Then they pulled up to the guard booth as the gate came back down, blocking them in.

Riel hugged herself. The awning above seemed to press in toward her, and her heart pounded so desperately that her vision flickered. She took a deep breath and pulled out her fake passport, handing it over to Evan, the cover slick with sweat from her palm.

Evan put the car in park and gave her a reassuring smile. Then he rolled down the tinted window.

"Good evening," Evan said jovially, handing the

passports out to the tall, wiry man at the booth. Definitely not Mishmash's guy. Riel took another breath, wiping the sweat from her forehead. *Keep calm. If you're nervous, it just makes it worse. These guys can smell fear, like dogs.* She concentrated hard on relaxing, and felt her heartbeat slow somewhat.

The border guard peered at them with cold, rheumy eyes the color of smoke. He glanced down at the passports, flipping them open, then walked back to his booth, taking his radio from his hip and muttering something into it.

"What is he saying?" Riel hissed.

"I don't know, I can't hear." He reached out to take her hand, squeezing it and shooting her a smile. "Don't worry, everything's okay."

The guard came back to the window. "I'm going to need you two to step out of the car," he said.

The sweat seemed to freeze on Riel's body.

"Is there a problem?" Evan asked. His voice was steady, politely confused.

"Just step out of the car please," the guard repeated.

Evan gave her a short, loaded glance, and Riel reached deep inside herself, finding calm there beneath the panic. *You can get through this. You can get out of this. Don't freak out.* They both unbuckled their seatbelts and climbed out of the car into the dry, balmy air.

The floodlights under the awning seemed unbearably bright. A breeze gusted, blowing her hair and bringing the smell of sage and exhaust. Riel breathed it deep. She was determined to stay free, to not get locked up again where she couldn't feel the wind on her face.

Another man approached her from the building off to the side of the checkpoint, a tall, broad-shouldered, Hispanic guy, and Riel smiled at him, putting as much charisma into it as she could. She saw a ghost of a smile soften his strong jaw in response before he caught himself and his expression sobered.

"Good evening," he said. "*Buenas tardes.*"

"Hi," Riel said.

The man walked around to the other side of the car, getting one of the passports from the other guard, who was standing with Evan. The guards exchanged a couple words, but Riel couldn't hear what they were saying over the noise of the car engines. The Hispanic guard came back around to her, his sharp eyes darting from the passport to her face. "What's your name?" he asked.

"Nora Mejia," she said.

"Your date and place of birth?"

She told him the date and place on the passport, glad she'd memorized them.

The guard studied the document, flipping through pages. She could hear Evan talking calmly behind her, something about San Diego and the beach. The Hispanic guard looked back up at her face. "What brought you to Mexico today?" he asked.

She shrugged perkily, bouncing on the balls of her feet to make her boobs jiggle. She saw the man's gaze slip down to her cleavage for a split second before he pulled it back to her face. "We just went to the beach," she said. "I'd never been to Mexico, and I wanted to go."

"Ah," the guy said. "Where do you live?"

"San Diego." She gave him the address on her fake driver's license. She'd memorized that too.

"You live in San Diego, but you've never been to Mexico?"

"Just moved there. I lived in Seattle before." The story rose to her lips as if it were the truth.

He studied her face, then jerked his chin toward Evan behind her. "This guy your boyfriend?"

Riel rolled her eyes theatrically, leaning her hips toward the guard a little. "Yeah."

She saw the man's lips twitch and one of his eyebrows creep up. His eyes skimmed over her body.

"Okay," he said. "Just hold up a second. Don't go anywhere."

He walked around the car, and he and his friend went in the booth, talking to each other in low voices and glancing at the passports. She and Evan exchanged a look over the hood of the car. He gave her a brief, reassuring smile, his hands in his pockets, his shoulders loose, though she knew him well enough to see the nervousness behind the act.

Both guys came out of the booth. They pulled flashlights out of their belts and shone them through the windows of the car, walking around the vehicle and scanning the inside. Riel sent up a silent prayer that the guns were well-hidden under the seats. When the guard asked Evan to pop the trunk, she prayed that the secret compartment was sealed up completely.

She wondered if there was enough coke in there to get her a life sentence. It would be her second offense while she was still on probation for the first, and she'd get another charge for the fake documents, since once they took her fingerprints they'd know who she was. There were a hell of a lot of drugs in that car, and smuggling across the border was a serious crime.

The two guards lingered over their task, murmuring to each other, prodding every corner of the vehicle with the beams of their flashlights, and Riel began to feel sick to her stomach. *Keep cool.* Her gaze found Evan's again, and he stuck his tongue out at her, crossing his eyes. Warmth flooded her, and she felt a smile rise to her lips. He grinned in response.

We've got to get out of this. I don't want to be locked up, away from him. Her smile faded, and Evan's did too. He held her gaze, the same thought seemingly passing silently between them.

The guards exchanged a couple more words, putting the flashlights back in their holsters. The blonde guy strutted toward Evan, and the Hispanic guy came toward her, his steps quick and purposeful. *This is it,* Riel thought, her heart in her throat.

The guy smiled. He handed her back her passport. "Okay, Miss Mejia. Sorry for the inconvenience. You're good to go."

Relief flooded her. She smiled back. "Thanks."

"Have a good evening," he said.

"You too."

Evan was smiling at the other guard, who was

retreating to his booth. He and Riel climbed back in the car and buckled their seatbelts. The automatic gate lifted, and Evan put the car in drive, rolling through the gate.

They hit the open road, back in California again. Both of them heaved a simultaneous sigh. Riel felt light and giddy, and she laughed. "What the fuck was *that?*"

Evan laughed too, but his expression was clouded. "I have no idea. That was fucked. Something was up. I'm surprised they let us go."

They looked at one another, and their hands clasped over the console. Riel knew he was thinking the same thing she was: they'd been lucky this time, but if they kept this up, it was only a matter of time before they were dead or in jail.

Chapter Ten

Mishmash listened to their tale soberly, stroking his mustache, then pulled out his phone and started texting. "I don't know what the hell happened," he said, his face pale. "Fat Matt told me he'd be working yesterday, seven to two, and never sent me a message saying otherwise."

"And it was weird," Riel said. "They had no real reason to pull us out of the car anyway, right?"

"Yeah, it did seem weird," Evan said. "It's like they were waiting for us."

Mishmash frowned, tapping his phone against his knee. "I'm really sorry that happened. Working for me isn't usually like this, Riel."

"I'll vouch for that," Evan said. "Mishmash usually has everything laid out smooth like a slip-and-slide."

Mishmash looked at the screen of his phone again. He sighed. "Anyway, I'll make double sure it doesn't happen again. I won't send you on another run until I've got it all figured out." He glanced around the hotel room. "How long you have this

123

place for?"

"Just one more night," Evan said. "We're going to look for an apartment." He smiled at Riel, taking her hand.

"How about a house?" Mishmash said, and they both looked at him. "I just had one of my rentals come open. Little two-bedroom, has a yard and everything. It's in an okay neighborhood. I think you'd like it."

Evan raised his eyebrows. "How much?"

Mishmash grinned. "For you two lovebirds, thirteen hundred a month."

Evan and Riel exchanged a glance. "That's not bad," Evan said.

Mishmash slapped his palms against his knees. "Let's go look at it, see what you think."

Evan and Riel exchanged another glance, and Evan shrugged. "Sure, why not?"

They headed out into the warm night, transferring the product from the Mustang to Mishmash's little Honda before climbing into their cars. Riel and Evan followed the Honda out of the parking lot and onto the highway.

"Why do you think he's giving us such a deal on a house?" Riel mused.

"My theory is he wants us to do some dealing too, and he just wants us by the balls a little tighter."

Riel rubbed the back of her neck. "Or maybe it's just a complete dump."

"Could be. We're about to see, I guess."

They pulled off at an exit, entering a quiet residential neighborhood. Then Evan frowned at the rearview mirror. "Are we being followed?"

Riel glanced behind them, and saw the headlights of what looked like an SUV and at least one smaller car behind it. "I don't—" she began to say, adrenaline numbing her tongue.

The SUV turned its brights on and revved up fast behind them, just as two other cars sped around it. One of them skidded to a halt in front of Mishmash's car, which fishtailed into an angled stop. Evan slammed the brakes, just barely missing the Honda as he also screeched to a stop. The third car pulled up beside them, the windows down, and Riel got a glimpse of faces, a flash of something silver.

Gunshots rang out. Riel screamed and ducked. Rapid-fire pistol shots. *Crack, crack, crack.*

Evan cursed and pushed her down, her head smacking the dashboard. They both slid off their seats crouched in the tight space under the dash, a tangle of awkward limbs on the floorboards. She could see Evan fishing under his seat for their guns.

"Did they get Mishmash?" she said, her voice a squeaky whisper. "Those shots were up there."

She could see his eyes glinting in the reflected headlight glow. "I don't fucking know. Where are the goddamn guns? There—"

More pistol shots. Riel screamed again as both the passengers' and driver's side windows of Evan's Mustang shattered, huge chunks of tempered glass falling onto her back and shoulders as she crouched against the glove box.

"You okay?" Evan yelped, his eyes wide.

"Yeah, you?" She could hear shouting outside,

caught the words, "*A la chingada madre...*"

"I'm fine. Here." He pressed a pistol into her sweaty palm, both of them cramped awkwardly with no room to maneuver.

The gun felt good in her trembling hand, but she couldn't see anything outside. Her exposed back prickled.

Then she gasped sharply as footsteps crunched outside. A man, silhouetted strangely in the bright headlights, appeared at the driver's window. Riel saw a gun come up, gleaming.

"This is from Isaias," he said.

Crack. The shot exploded against her eardrums. Adrenaline screamed through her and she scrambled to get her gun up, her hand caught against the gear shift, her arm cramped against the console. She aimed at the silhouette and fired. One, two, three times. Her ears rang as her hearing went dead. The silhouette disappeared from the window, but she couldn't tell where it had gone. Her eyes were blinded with tears.

She heard Evan gasp. He made a strange gurgling noise. Fear shot through her. "Evan!" she screamed, her voice dull and quiet in her damaged ears. More shouting outside. Sirens. "Evan?"

He stirred, then collapsed awkwardly against the dash, his face turned away from her. "Riel, shit," he said, his voice a hoarse whisper that barely cut through the fuzz in her ears. She reached out to him with her free hand, the other one still clutching the gun.

Her hand met flesh that was sticky and slick with blood. She screamed and shook him, and he

126

wobbled limply, sliding down further. "Evan!" she wailed.

"I think he got me," he muttered weakly. Dully, she saw the red and blue flash of police lights joining the glare of headlights. She thought she heard tires squealing away. She huddled, shivering, in the space between the seat and the dash, not feeling the pain in her cramped knees. She sobbed Evan's name, over and over. But he didn't respond again.

Chapter Eleven

Riel huddled under the wool blanket the EMTs had given her. "Miss Mejia, I know this is hard, and I'm sorry to have to put you through this, but we just have a few more questions."

She stared dully at the cop in front of her, his face illuminated by the flashing lights of a dozen patrol cars. His name was Officer Norton, and it seemed like he'd been asking her the same questions over and over for hours.

"Please," she said, "I just want to go to the hospital. I want to be with Theodore."

"He's with the medics, miss, there's nothing you can do for him right now. He's in the best hands. Now, you're certain you didn't know these people who shot him? Never seen them anywhere before?"

"I only saw the one guy, and not that well," she said. "He said something about an Isaias. I don't know an Isaias. I think they had the wrong people." She squeezed her eyes shut, her words choking her. Other cops swarmed around, their radios squawking. Some were talking to the residents of

128

the houses around them, others were examining the crime scene.

Mishmash, Evan, and three other men had been taken away in ambulances, including the guy Riel herself had shot, the one who had hurt Evan. She had to figure they wouldn't have taken any of them away if they were dead, but she couldn't get anyone to tell her what was going on. *Evan has to still be alive.* She pulled the blanket tighter around her. Riel had to keep them from arresting her so she could get to the hospital.

"And the man driving the car in front of you?" Officer Norton persisted, his voice cutting through her thoughts. "Did you know him?"

"No," Riel said weakly. "We'd just pulled off this way, looking for a place to turn around. We were going to a restaurant and got lost."

She pressed her chin to her chest, swallowing her tears. There were so many holes in her story, there was no way she was staying out of jail, but she just wanted to see Evan first. "Please," she said. "I need to get to the hospital."

He laid a hand on her shoulder, and Riel looked at it as if the officer's hand were a rare bird that had just landed there. "Okay, miss," the cop said. "I think I can give you a ride there. Just let me talk to a couple people. Will you wait here?"

She nodded jerkily, wiping her eyes, her brow furrowing. She watched him walk over and have a muttered conversation with one of his colleagues, who was examining the Mustang with a flashlight. Was this a trick?

After a minute, Officer Norton came back.

"Okay, Miss Mejia. Let's go to the hospital and check on your boyfriend, okay?"

"Thank you." Relief and dread flooded her at once. "Thank you so much."

She followed him over to his patrol car, which was parked at a haphazard angle across the road, its lights still flashing. He opened the front passenger door for her, and she climbed in. He was letting her ride in the front. Her heart pounded in her sore ears.

The door shut, sealing her in with the serious clunk that only happens in cop cars. Then Officer Norton climbed into the driver's seat. Riel could see the pistol in his utility belt, and got a pang of irrational fear. *He's going to shoot me.* Her chest tightened around her racing heart. Lights flashed behind her eyes, mingling with the strobe of the cruiser lights.

She tried to steady her breathing. He wasn't going to shoot her, not after he let her sit in the front of his car.

Officer Norton glanced sideways at her. "You okay?" His voice seemed loud in the quiet cabin.

She took another breath, her fear abating. "Y-yeah."

He gazed at her a moment longer. "That's some serious action you just saw there."

She didn't respond. She didn't know what to say.

The cop's lips twitched up slightly. "You did a good job on the guy that hurt your boyfriend. Pretty good shooting, especially considering what position you were in."

Riel winced, bile rising up in her throat. Why weren't they arresting her? She shot someone, with a hot gun. She shot someone..."I didn't want to kill...I was just trying to keep him from killing us—"

"I know you didn't. I'm sorry I brought it up. Buckle up, let's get out of here, okay?"

She nodded. He started the engine and spoke into his radio, telling the other officers where he was headed, but she barely heard. She was still wrapped in the blanket, but she awkwardly maneuvered the seatbelt around her torso.

They pulled away from the scene, the engine humming smoothly. The flashing patrol lights faded behind them, leaving them immersed in the over-bright glow of the many dashboard instruments. Riel felt lost and dizzy. She pressed her feet against the floorboards; she wished he would drive faster. What if Evan died before she got there? She clenched her teeth, pushing the thought away.

It was several blocks before Officer Norton spoke. "It's a tough life, being caught up this gang bullshit, if you'll excuse my language, miss."

Riel felt a pang of dread, and glanced at him sharply. "I'm not," she said. "I was just—"

"Mishmash happens to be a friend of mine," he said.

Riel just stared at the officer as he gazed stone-faced out the windshield. Her heart wriggled in her throat. "Who's Mishmash?"

He was silent for a moment longer, then he gave her a shrewd glance. "He told me a few days ago that he'd found someone who might be able to bring Isaias down. Now, I don't always see eye-to-eye with Mishmash, but he's pretty good at keeping things from getting out of hand around here. He's a good businessman, even if I don't like what he's selling. I can't blame a guy for wanting to make a living, I guess, is what I'm saying. We all do what we can to get by." He raised her eyebrows at her, his gaze darting between her and the road. She licked her lips and stayed silent.

He rubbed his nose with his fist and continued. "Isaias' people are the ones causing all the problems around here. I don't like being called to scenes like this one. If there's any way to stop stuff like that from happening, to keep people like you and your boyfriend from getting hurt, or worse, it would be irresponsible not to do it."

They pulled up in front of the hospital. Riel's heart raced, and her mouth was dry. She didn't know if this was a trap or not. She just wanted to see Evan. She wished none of this had happened. She hid her face in her hands.

Officer Norton shut off the engine, and she could feel him looking at her. "Listen, Miss Mejia. You seem like a good girl who doesn't deserve to be caught up in this bullcrap. But you shot a man tonight. I'm guessing we could find drugs in one or both vehicles if we looked hard enough. You know as well as I do that I should be taking you to the station, instead of here to the hospital to see your boyfriend. But I'd like us to work together."

She wiped her eyes with trembling hands and looked up at him. He smiled faintly.

"Let's go see how your boyfriend and Mishmash are doing, all right?"

She nodded, and they got out of the car.

The hospital lights seemed too bright, and the bustle of the ER waiting room was disorienting. Everyone looked up when they came in, a cop and a girl in a blanket with blood smudged on her face and hands.

They went to the information desk, and Officer Norton spoke to the woman there, asking after Theodore Anderson. Riel's stomach cramped up with dread as the woman looked him up on her computer, and Riel watched her face closely, terrified that she was going to wince or frown or give her a look, the look that said, *I don't want to have to be the one to tell her this, but he's dead.*

The woman's eyes skimmed the screen, the glow reflected in her eyes. She blinked. "Checked in an hour and a half ago. Gunshot wound to the neck and shoulder. He's still in the trauma unit."

Riel hugged herself. "What does that mean? Is he okay?"

The receptionist looked at her, and Riel saw very little pity in her face. "He's still being worked on. It will be a while before you can see him."

Riel nodded numbly, clutching her arms around her middle. The blanked slipped around her shoulders.

"What about Hilario Valencia?" Officer Norton said.

It took Riel a couple moments to realize that he must be talking about Mishmash. The receptionist started typing again, then cocked a penciled eyebrow. "Another gunshot wound." Her eyes darted to the cop's. "Been a rough night."

"Sure has, ma'am."

The woman's gaze skimmed the screen, and Riel's guts twisted. If he was dead, what would happen to her?

"He's out of critical care," the woman finally said. "Stable condition in the recovery ward."

"Can we visit him?" Norton asked.

"He may be asleep, but I don't see why not."

She gave them the room number, and Officer Norton and Riel headed for the elevators. On the way up, he adjusted the blanket around her shoulders. "It's going to be all right," he said.

She glanced up at him, tears leaking from her eyes.

"Listen, I…I'm no doctor, but I saw your boyfriend before they took him away. He had a hole in him, no joke, and he'd lost a lot of blood, but the EMTs got to him right away, and it didn't look like he was really hit bad. I mean, it didn't look like they got him where it counts."

Riel gazed at him hopefully, wanting to believe, but she thought she saw uncertainty in his eyes. Was this just part of his game, to get her guard down?

"Thank you," she said.

He nodded faintly. "Like I said, I'm not a medic, but I've been to enough of these scenes to know when it's a lost cause, and your boyfriend definitely wasn't." The doors opened. "Come on, let's see Mishmash."

They headed out into the hallways, where nurses wheeled carts and bustled around with clipboards. Their uniforms looked like prison clothes, and Riel had a dizzy moment of disorientation.

Mishmash was sleeping, being attended by a woman in a red frock. He looked strange and shrunken, his face grey. What Riel could see of his torso was covered in bandages and a hospital gown, which looked wrong on him. It made him look weak, and silly.

The nurse looked up as they walked in, her eyes going wide, then hooded when she saw Officer Norton's uniform.

"How is he doing?" Norton asked.

"You here to question him?" the nurse said.

"No, actually. Here on more of a personal call, for his friend Miss Mejia here." He patted Riel's shoulder.

The nurse's shoulders relaxed somewhat, her gaze seeking out Riel's. "He was apparently shot twice at close range. He may have some muscle damage, but otherwise he's fine. He's just sleeping. I'll have the doctor come in and give you a full report as soon as she can."

Riel nodded. The nurse left, and Riel and Norton sat down in the bedside chairs. As soon as the nurse left, Mishmash stirred, cracking an eye open. "She gone?"

Officer Norton chuckled. "You big faker."

"You can't knock out a man from Michoacán, even with two bullets and a liter of fentanyl." Mishmash tried to sit up, then winced, his face going even paler.

"Lay down, dude," Norton said. "You've just been cracked hard."

"Little pussy guns," Mishmash murmured. "Those boys can't afford good ones in my town."

He settled against the pillows, his eyes finding Riel's. "You okay?"

Riel nodded. "But Theodore…"

Mishmash's expression darkened, his gaze flicking to Norton's.

"He's still in surgery," the cop said.

Mishmash relaxed a little, but his face was still clouded with anger. "Those fucking *jotos*. I'd like to shove their balls down their fucking throats."

Riel hugged herself, wondering if Evan was out of surgery yet, if he were still alive. Would a nurse come find them if something happened?

Norton shifted in his seat, tugging at his slacks. "Well, that's why we're here, actually. To see what we can do about those *jotos*."

Mishmash caught Riel's eye again, a look passing between them. "Norton here's all right," he said. "You can trust him. You *should* trust him." He grinned. "Snortin' Norton. You can trust good old Snortin' Norton."

The cop shook his head, smirking. "They've got you laid out, man. You're talking bullshit."

"This is some good shit, the medical dope. I oughta get shot more often. But no, *m'ija*, I'm *en serio*. This cop's one of the good guys. He's on the right side of the law."

Norton shook his head again. His eyes darted nervously to the open doorway, and he got up, closed it, and sat back down, looking at Riel seriously. "We want you to work with us. We can offer good protection and resources. We need you to help us bring down Isaias."

Riel clutched her blanket, tears streaming down

her cheeks. "I just want Theodore to be okay. I can't think about anything else right now."

"He'll be okay," Norton said. "We need you to help us make sure nobody ever gets shot by that asshole and his thugs ever again. We're doing this for Theodore."

Riel hid her face in her hands, willing herself to stop trembling. "What can I do? Isaias hates me. I don't have an in with him. There's nothing I can offer you that would help."

"We have a plan, Nora," Norton said. "Or should I say, Gabriella." He raised his eyebrows at her.

Riel winced, and wiped her eyes. "What's the plan?"

Riel sat listening, chewing her cheek, as Officer Norton told her the plan. Meanwhile, Mishmash tapped the button for his automatic narcotics drip, humming under his breath.

"It's a good plan, right?" he said when the cop had finished.

Riel's brow furrowed. "But what about after? What happens to me and Evan after that?"

"You'll be immune from prosecution," Norton said. "We'll even work with you on the probation violation. You'll be off scot-free."

She stomped her feet. "But for how long?" Both men watched her silently, wide-eyed. "I never wanted to get involved in this drug bullshit in the first place," she said. "Isaias made me. I want to have a normal life. I want to go to college. I want to get a little house with Evan, and have…and have a cat, you know. A normal life." She felt heat rise to her cheeks.

A hazy sentimental grin spread over Mishmash's face. He tapped his painkiller button again. "A cat. *Que lindo.*" Norton was gazing at her almost curiously. Then Mishmash sighed. "How about this," he said. "You do this thing for us, you get free rent on that house we were going to look at for two years, and I'll give your man a job at one of my car lots or something. A real job, good money, all above-board. You can go to college. I'll even buy you a kitten." He grinned. "Sound good?"

Riel sat stiffly as both men gazed at her. Finally, she nodded. "But only if Evan is okay. If something…" She flinched, sending a fresh wave of tears down her cheeks. "If something happens to him, all deals are off."

Mishmash nodded. "We have a bargain." He tried to hold out his hand toward her, then winced and grunted. "I can't hold up my arm, mama."

Riel stood and went over and gently shook his hand, which was cold and sweaty.

"Just make sure that cat doesn't tear up my carpets," he said.

She gave him a teary smile. "Deal."

Chapter Twelve

They went back down to the waiting room after talking to Mishmash's doctor. Norton had another conversation with the woman at the help desk while Riel found a seat near a tired-looking young woman, who was trying to contain a grumpy toddler with a huge, red lump on his head.

The young mother gave Norton a suspicious sideways glance as he sat down with a sigh next to Riel, and Riel had a moment of dizziness. It seemed like this had been the longest day of her life, and it somehow culminated in her hanging out in a hospital, on friendly terms with a cop.

"They'll come get us when your boyfriend is out of surgery," he said.

Riel nodded, staring at her knees.

They sat forever. To Riel, it felt like the sun should be up, like hours and hours had passed, but according to the clock it was only a little after eleven. The sky beyond the windows remained dark, the glass reflecting the scene within the waiting room in a warped parody. Riel's thoughts jumped around like agitated monkeys, and it wasn't until Officer Norton came back with a plastic-wrapped ham sandwich and a Coke that she realized she was trembling with hunger.

She fumbled with the packaging so badly that Norton took the food back from her. He unwrapped the sandwich, popped the tab on the soda, and returned them.

"You've had quite a night," he said.

She nodded, the soda sloshing in the can. She tried to steady herself.

He jerked his chin toward the food. "Eat something. I swear it helps."

"I'm not hungry."

"Eat it anyway."

She stared at the smashed ham and cheese. Nothing had ever looked more unappetizing, but she took a bite. It didn't taste bad, but it felt weird in her mouth. She swallowed it down her dry throat, washed it down with soda, and looked sideways at the cop, who was regarding her curiously. Her brow wrinkled.

"Have you ever…" She licked her lips, frowning, and he smiled faintly.

"Have I ever shot a man?" he said quietly, and she curled in on herself, nodding. He passed a hand over his forehead. "In fact, I have. Once."

She examined his face. He stared distantly at the far wall, shifting in his chair. "Line of duty, about two years ago. Guy came at me with a gun, and I didn't even think, I just let loose. After, I found out the gun wasn't loaded. It was some kid, twenty-three years old. I thought he was whacked out on

PCP or something, but he was actually schizophrenic." The corners of his eyes crinkled as a look of pain passed over his face. "I didn't know any of that. Wish I had."

"Did he die?"

Norton nodded, then sat up and smiled jerkily. "I still see him fall, see the look on his face. Dream about it."

"You didn't know," Riel said. "Anyone would have done the same thing. You thought he was going to shoot you."

"And what you did tonight, anyone would have done that too," he said. "I checked, and the guy you got is messed up pretty bad, but they say he'll live. He'll be in jail a long, long time, though."

Riel took a deep and shuddering breath. It felt good to talk about it, and it kept her mind off of Evan. She wanted to ask Officer Norton how he'd gotten involved with Mishmash, but knew she'd better not, not here in the waiting room with the young mother shooting them curious looks.

The wait dragged on and on. The hand on the clock passed midnight, then twelve thirty. They called the young mother, and others. The waiting room started to empty out, and still they sat. Riel ate half her sandwich, the can of soda going warm in her hand, and began to suspect that they were just stalling, not wanting to tell her, *I'm sorry, Miss Mejia, but there was nothing we could do.*

When a white-coated doctor finally approached them at a quarter to one, Riel felt a sick wave of adrenaline that threatened to bring the ham and cheese back up again.

"Miss Mejia?" the doctor said, and Riel nodded, fighting back her hope and fear.

The doctor smiled. "Mr. Anderson is out of surgery. He's stable, and resting."

"Oh my god," Riel breathed, hiding her face in her hands, her cheeks wet with tears.

"He'll have scarring, but he'll be fine." Riel shook with laughter and sobs as the doctor spoke. "Do you want to see him?"

Riel wasn't sure her legs would carry her, but she got up. Norton kept his arm around her as they trotted down the hall, up in the elevators, and to Evan's room.

They found him grey and unconscious, wrapped in bandages, but his chest was still rising and falling underneath the thin hospital sheets.

Riel took his cold, limp hand. He looked different, like Mishmash had: his cheeks were sunken and his complexion was grey, but it was Evan. Her eyes blurred with tears, and she pressed his hand to her forehead.

"I told you he'd be okay," Norton said, but Riel couldn't answer.

Riel sat by his bedside as he slept, staring at his face, watching him breathe. Nurses and doctors came in and out, checking his IVs and the monitors, and at two in the morning Norton prepared to leave, telling her he'd be back later.

"I'd tell you not to take off on me, but I don't think that's an issue anyway," he said.

"No. I'm not going anywhere."

Norton left. Riel realized she had nowhere else to go even if she wanted to, no idea what happened after this, but she didn't care. There was nowhere else she would be right now.

The sky outside the window was still dark, and the ward was fairly quiet. *We're going to have a house, and legal money, and a cat. All I have to do is bring down Isaias.*

Her shoulders slumped as she thought about it. But she took a deep breath, let it out. *I can do it. I'll bring that asshole down, for Lizette, and Laina...and for him.* She squeezed Evan's hand.

As the sky began to brighten beyond the windows, Riel fell asleep, curled up in a chair at his bedside, still holding his hand.

***

Riel startled awake. She had a moment of bleary disorientation. She was cramped and sore, and sunlight streamed into a room that was too white.

"I was wondering if you were ever going to wake up."

Riel gasped and jerked upright. "Evan!"

He smiled weakly. A nurse was there, adjusting his bed into a sitting position, placing a tray of food in front of him. She glanced at Riel and smiled. "You his wife?"

Riel avoided Evan's eyes. "Girlfriend."

"He's going to have trouble lifting his arms," the nurse said. "Can you help him eat?"

"Of course."

The nurse left, and Riel scooted closer, picking up the plastic spork.

"How's Mishmash?" he asked.

143

She nodded faintly. "He's okay. Better off than you. They got him in the shoulder, but the cops showed up." Riel stared at the plate, and she wrinkled her nose. "Is this supposed to be meatloaf?"

He smiled, and her heart twisted. He looked so weak. "It might be, or it could be a misplaced surgical sponge. Who cares, I'd eat from a Tijuana trashcan at this point."

"Ew," Riel said, grinning. "Are you really that hungry?" She pried off a lump of the meat.

"I just feel like I need to eat, you know?"

"You lost a lot of blood." She held the fork up. "Here comes the airplane."

He snorted, opening his mouth. She stuck the food in, and his brow scrunched up as he chewed, his eyes darting to the doorway. "So, why aren't we in jail, anyway? I mean, that was a pretty sketchy situation, to say the least. I figured we'd at least be held for questioning. Or, better yet, why aren't we dead?"

As Riel poked bits of green beans, meat, and mashed potatoes in his mouth, she filled him in on what had happened after he'd lost consciousness. She started with how she'd shot the man who had shot him, which caused him to give her a long, dark look.

"I'm sorry, Riel."

She shrugged. "I did what I had to do, I guess."

"This job freakin' sucks. But now I'm *really* curious as to why we're not in jail, or at least you."

So she told him about Officer Norton, and the deal that she'd cut with him and Mishmash. Evan tried to sit up straight, but just succeeded in making the color drain from his face. "No," he said, his voice hoarse with pain.

"Evan—"

"No way, Riel. *I'll* do it, but there's no chance in hell I'm sending you to…and with that asshole…" He let out a breath through gritted teeth as he readjusted himself in the bed.

"Are you okay? Do you want me to call the doctor?"

"Don't worry about it. But you're changing the subject."

She pressed her lips together. "I'm sorry, Evan. But this needs to be done if we're ever going to escape this bullshit life, and I'm the only one who can do it."

He squinted at her silently. She spooned up a lump of Jell-O, held it up for him, but he turned his face away. "You're not the only one who could do this, Riel. I could too."

"You know that's not true. Isaias wouldn't buy that for a minute. Come on. Eat your Jell-O."

He grudgingly took a bite, and she wiped his lips with a napkin. "I can handle this," she said.

"I know you can, Riel. You're tough as shit. I just don't want you to have to handle it, that's all."

"But you know I'm the best one for the job. And when it's all over, we can live happily ever after."

Her eyes searched his, and he smiled, his hand creeping over to take hers. "You really want to settle down with me?" he asked.

Warmth bloomed in Riel's breast. She smiled. "I really want to settle down with the cat, but it'd be nice to have you around too."

He laughed, but his eyes were anguished. Then he sighed, the strength seeming to drain out of him. "Just…just don't get hurt, okay?"

"I won't," she said, hoping it was true.

Chapter Thirteen

Riel curled up on the secondhand sofa next to Evan, who sat carefully against the pillows, his shoulder still bandaged. In the armchairs across from them were Officer Norton and a man from the FBI by the name of Christopher McCormack.

Chris leaned forward over his bony knees. He reminded Riel of a stick figure. Even his beady eyes and thin lips seemed sketched on.

"Whatever you tell Isaias to get back in his good graces, that's up to you," he said. "But everything hinges on that. If he doesn't believe you, this whole plan is going to fall apart."

Riel nodded, clutching her knees.

"After you get him to accept you back, it won't get much easier," Chris continued. "You're still going to have to play a pretty convincing part to get him to take the bait. These situations can get dangerous pretty fast if people start to suspect it's a setup."

Evan frowned, a muscle in his jaw twitching. "But you're going to protect her, right? You're not going to use her like some sort of pawn to do your work for you without any sort of backup?"

"She'll be protected at all times," he said. "We'll have multiple agents following her every move and staying as close by as possible, ready to offer aid. However, if it becomes necessary for us to become involved before the transaction has happened, it will be harder for us to guarantee her safety in the future, because Isaias will be still out on the streets, and not in prison where he belongs."

Riel's hands tightened into fists. "I'll make sure he goes to jail."

Evan gave her a desperate look, then stared at Chris with his lips pressed together. Eventually, he nodded. "If anyone can do this, she can. But just make sure you keep her safe."

"We will," Chris said. "And this is how we'll do it." He opened his satchel and took out a cell phone, which he gave to Riel. She turned it over in her hands, running her fingers along its edges. It was a brand new iPhone in a floral print case. "All calls on this phone will be monitored," Chris said. "Not only that, but it has a very sensitive microphone in it that will pick up any noise within a fifty-foot radius and transmit it to our command unit. They'll be recording everything, so it's absolutely imperative that you have this device on you at all times when you're speaking with Isaias. It also has a tracking device installed, so we'll know where you are and can be ready to respond if you need our assistance."

"How will you know for sure when she needs help?" Evan asked. "It's not like she can just yell,

'FBI, I need your help'. She'd be dead before you got there." He winced, passing his hand across his face.

"There are several ways you can alert us that you need help," Chris said, looking at Riel. "One of those ways is verbally. Repeat the phrase, 'Don't do this' three times in a row. The microphone will pick it up and we'll come for you. In most situations where you'd need us to come in, saying that three times wouldn't seem too out of context."

"Sure," Riel said, tugging at her hair. She imagined Isaias backing her against the wall with a gun to her head.

"You can also dial three-three-three-pound if you need help," Chris continued. "That will bring backup immediately. And there's also these." He reached into his satchel again and came out with a small box.

Riel took it from him, and opened it. Inside were a pair of round earrings; they looked like onyx set in white gold.

"For me? You shouldn't have," she said.

Chris grinned wryly. "They're cameras. Each one has a tiny lens behind the 'stone.' If you get into trouble, we'll probably be able to see that and make the call whether we should come in. But you can also alert us by tapping on one of the earrings, two sets of three taps. *Tap, tap, tap, pause, tap, tap, tap.* Got it?"

Riel nodded, tapping on her earlobes.

"The battery pack is hidden in the setting and should be good for several months," Chris said. "Hopefully this mission won't take longer than a

149

few days, but if things go haywire and it ends up taking longer, we'll work something out to get you replacements."

Riel pulled the earrings from their case, turning them over in her hands. The bases were very thick, and they were heavier than she expected. Her spine seared with adrenaline when she thought of what was to come. Would she have the courage to pull this off? She didn't know.

And what if it really did drag on for months? Could she stand it?

She felt a hand on her knee, and looked up into Evan's green eyes.

Riel squared her shoulders and smiled at him, and he smiled back hesitantly. *I can do this. I'll do it for him, so we can be together happily ever after.*

She picked up the phone again. "I'm going to call Isaias now. Is that okay?"

Officer Norton and Chris exchanged a glance, and Evan's hand tightened on her knee.

"Now?" Evan said. "Not now, Riel. You have to give this more thought."

Riel shook her head. "No, I don't. I know what I'm going to say, and if I put it off, I'm just going to have time to over-think it and get scared."

Evan winced with pain as he leaned towards her. "Riel—"

"I've got to do this, Evan. It's the only way. And it's better to just get it over with than sit around worrying about it."

They exchanged a long look. Finally, he nodded, and she thought she saw him blinking away tears.

Riel took a deep breath and picked up the phone.

She glanced up at Chris, who was looking at her proudly. "It has a San Diego area code?" she asked. "This phone?"

"Yes. It'll come up on caller ID just like any other phone from this area. It won't say 'FBI Informant,' we promise," he said dryly, grinning.

She stared down at the screen. Luckily, she had Isaias' number memorized from all that time in prison, when his was the only number he'd wanted her to call. Her fingers trembled as she dialed it, and she had to backspace a couple of times.

She gulped air as it rang. Would he answer if he didn't recognize the number? Maybe, or maybe not. Should she leave a message?

After the fourth ring, when she was beginning to lose hope, there was a click, then a pause. "Hello?"

Riel felt sweat pop out on her forehead, her stomach lurching dangerously. She hadn't realized how much she hated hearing his voice. "Isaias?"

The line rumbled as he snorted into the receiver. "Is this *Riel?*"

"Y-yes."

"I can't fucking believe it. How do you have the guts to call me?"

She clutched the phone in her sweaty palm. "Isaias, I—"

"You really think you can come crawling back after you fucked up so bad, ditched me for that dipshit *joto* you're all wet for? No way, Riel. *Vete a la chingada.*"

She half expected him to hang up, but he didn't; she could still hear him breathing on the other end. For all his bluster, he wanted to hear what she had

151

to say, and she gathered courage from that.

"Isaias, it's not like you think," she said. Her voice shook, and she let it. "I was pissed off at you, I'll admit it, but I didn't actually want to leave. I didn't want it to turn out like this."

"What bullshit is this? *Que soy menso*? You really think I'll believe you?"

"Please, just listen."

"I'm listening, Riel. Go ahead and say your lies."

She squeezed Evan's hand, trying to bring her heartbeat under control. "After you and I got in that fight, I ran out of there. I was pissed off. I wasn't really thinking. I found some guy on the street, borrowed his phone, and called Evan."

"You weren't thinking, all right," Isaias said.

"What was I supposed to do? You think I wanted to go back there? You *hit* me, Isaias! You were being a total *puto*."

Her heart pounded in her ears at the silence on the other end. Evan and the two cops were looking at her wide-eyed. This was a gamble, maybe, but this act wouldn't be believable if she weren't pissed off.

"Maybe I overreacted a little," Isaias finally said. "But after the bitchy things you said…"

"I shouldn't have said them. But I didn't want to work there. I didn't want to be a whore. And you're my sister's husband, Isaias. I love Lizette more than anything in the world, and how do you think it makes me feel that I want…" Riel swallowed the vomit that crept up her throat. "I mean, I can't fuck you no matter how much…" Evan's jaw twitched and he clutched her hand so hard it hurt, but she

152

rolled her eyes at him.

Isaias was silent for a moment, and when he spoke there was a sly smile in his voice. "I knew you wanted it," he said. "I knew you were just *haciendote la dura.*"

"It would be wrong, Isaias. And how could you even want me? You have Lizette, and she's so much prettier. She's always been the pretty one."

"No, Riel," Isaias purred. "Don't get me wrong, your sister is beautiful, but you're so much hotter. Those luscious tits of yours, and that round little ass. Come back to me, Riel, and I'll show you how gorgeous I think you are."

"But my sister…"

"What she doesn't know won't hurt her. Besides, you'd be doing her a favor. With the kids, she's too tired to fuck anyway."

Riel winced. "I want to come back," she said. "Will you promise not to hit me anymore?"

"I'll be gentle, Riel, I promise. I'll be real gentle, until you tell me you want it harder."

She fought back her nausea. "Really? You'll take me back? And you'll be nice? Because I don't want to stay here anymore."

A note of curiosity tempered his sickeningly flirtatious tone. "Why? What's going on there? They treating you bad?"

She met Evan's eyes, trying to give him a reassuring look. "Evan's got me working for some asshole named Mishmash, but it's a bad scene. We got shot at. Evan and Mishmash got hurt bad. They missed me, but now the police are all up in our shit. The guy doesn't have it together, and I'm…it's scary. I don't think I can take it anymore."

Isaias laughed. "Mishmash, huh? I'd wondered where you'd gone." Riel chewed her lip. *Yeah, right, you wondered.* "That guy's a loser, Riel," Isaias said. "You're gonna end up dead working for that *vato.*"

"Yeah, I know," Riel said. "And both he and Evan are being dicks. They want me to do…a bunch of stuff that I don't want to do, like I'm their little bitch or something."

"Aw, babe, come back home. I promise I'll take good care of you."

"Really? Will you take me back?"

"Yeah. I'll treat you like a princess. None of that getting shot at crap. You know I've got my business in hand up here."

Riel wiped the sweat from her neck. "Okay, but I'll need money to come up. They're not letting me keep any money."

"I'll buy you a ticket," he said. "No worries."

"Thank you, Isaias." She took a deep breath. "And I think I have something else that will make me coming back worth your while."

There was a moment of silence. "Oh, really?"

Riel smiled to herself and closed her eyes, imagining Isaias getting the shit beat out of him in prison.

Chapter Fourteen

When she hung up, Evan was pale, his fingers clutching the worn upholstery of the couch so hard Riel worried he'd tear holes in it.

"That was really good work," Chris said, his eyebrows raised. "I don't think he suspected a thing."

"Isaias is a dipshit," Riel said.

"Isaias is no dummy," Norton said, "but every man has his weaknesses." He was smirking, but she could see the deep respect behind it.

"We'll make sure that everything is ready for you up north," Chris said, closing his briefcase. He got to his feet, and so did Norton. Both of them shook her hand. "You ready? How you holding up?" Chris asked.

"I'm okay," Riel said. "I'll get this done."

Chris nodded, and Officer Norton smiled.

"We'll take care of a few things, then we'll be back this evening before you catch your bus to Portland," Norton said.

"Okay, thank you," Riel said.

155

They left, closing the door and the iron security gate behind them.

Mishmash's little rental house was plunged into sudden silence, and Riel was left facing a furious-looking Evan.

"How could you say that shit?" he asked. He pounded the couch cushions, then winced at the pain in his shoulder. "You're going to fuck him, Riel? Is this little deal worth that?"

"I'm not going to fuck him."

"How do you think you're going to get out of it? He's going to expect it, after what you said. If you refuse again, he's going to get violent. And then what? Those agents won't be close enough to help you."

Riel stared at him, her fists unclenching as she saw the tears in his eyes. "Evan, don't worry."

"How can you expect me not to worry?" His voice broke. "I can't stand the thought of you...and if he hits you again..." His nostrils flared. "I'll kill that fucker, Riel, I really will. They'll have me in jail because I'll rip his fucking dick off and shove it so far down his throat he'll choke to death."

She scooted over and put her arms around him, feeling the cords of his tense muscles under his shirt. His lips were pressed together, but they relaxed as she kissed him. "I promise, I'll handle it," she murmured. "I won't have to fuck him. I have a plan."

"Riel..." He slid his good hand around her waist, his stiff posture loosening slightly.

"I'm smarter than Isaias."

"I know you are, but—"

"I need to do this. It's the only way we'll be able to escape this business and be safe."

"I could figure out another way if you'd just give me time."

"Isaias would have us killed by then, or something else would happen. This is the opportunity of a lifetime, and I'd be stupid not to take it."

"What if this goes wrong? What if you get hurt? I wouldn't be able to go on living, knowing that I sat here safe, not doing anything."

"What I'm doing now is safer than running drugs. I'll have police backup. You heard them. And, Evan, you were just in the hospital for three days because you got frigging *shot*. You expect *me* to just sit here and not do anything, when there's something I can do to make us safe?"

He scowled, his gaze dropping to his lap.

She brushed the curls from his pale forehead and kissed him lightly. "It'll be okay," she said.

But she couldn't help but share his worries.

***

Officer Norton and Chris came back over that afternoon, going over the plan with her again and double-checking that her equipment was functioning correctly. Then they helped her load her luggage into a taxi. Neither of them went with her, nor did Evan; they were worried Isaias might have a lookout stationed there to make sure she arrived alone.

The lawmen shook her hand and patted her on

the back, and Evan clung to her desperately as she stood at the open door to the cab. "Be careful, Riel," he said. "Please."

"I will," she said.

Evan pulled away, his mouth twisted up against his grief. "I love you."

A smile spread over her face. "I love you too, Evan."

She kissed him one last time, wanting to preserve the memory of his lips on hers as a talisman against fear and bad luck. Then she climbed into the cab and shut the door, and before she knew it, they were driving away. She watched out the back window as Evan's hunched form grew smaller in the driveway.

Riel tore her gaze away and faced the front, fighting down the lump in her throat. She wondered if she'd ever see him again.

"Bus station, right?" the driver said, and she nodded, wiping her eyes.

"Going on a trip?" he asked.

"You might say that." Riel crossed her arms and gazed out the window. The driver took the hint and didn't ask any more questions.

The bus ride was painfully long and boring. She was stuck all the way to Medford next to a woman who wouldn't stop talking about how her boyfriend had kicked her out of the house. "He said I was a tweaker," she said for the billionth time, sucking on her loose dentures. "I'm not a goddamn tweaker. I hate those motherfuckers with a purple passion. His sister is just telling him that bullshit because she's a fucking bitch who can't handle the fact that I won't put up with her crap like everyone else does. I'm a blunt person, I don't beat around the fucking bush, and when someone is being a goddamn cunt, I feel it's my obligation to let them know about it."

"Uh huh," Riel said. She stared out the window at twilight falling over the oak-covered hills, wishing Isaias had enough class to buy her a plane ticket.

It was the afternoon of the next day when Riel finally emerged from the bus, sore and extremely grubby-feeling, to find Isaias waiting for her in the station.

"Hey, Riel," he said.

His muscular arms were crossed over his chest, and he had a smug look as his eyes skimmed her body. Riel immediately went stiff under that gaze, and had a moment of panic. *I can't do this. I can't stand the sight of him. I can't pretend to like him.* She stood there a moment, dizzy, but then she gathered up her courage. *I have to do this. For Evan. For Lizette.*

Riel felt the smile rise to her lips as if she were wearing someone else's face. "Hey," she said.

He took her suitcase from her, glancing at her out of the corner of his eye as they headed out the door to the parking lot. "SoCal made you all tan. You look hot."

She had to keep herself from scowling as she hugged herself against the damp chill of the Portland spring. "I can't look that good, I've been stuck on a bus for twenty-six hours."

He grinned as he loaded her suitcase into the back of his SUV. "You'd definitely look better if you were cleaned up a bit, I won't lie, but you're still a spicy piece."

They climbed into the cab, and he reached into the backseat and handed her a paper sack. "You hungry?"

She blinked at him, then opened the sack and was hit in the face by a burst of delicious steam. "Oh my god, you went to Bud's?" She pulled out a carton and opened it. Fried chicken, mashed potatoes, okra, and coleslaw.

"I know their fried chicken is your favorite, and I figured you wouldn't have eaten much on your trip."

"Fank you, Isaiaff," Riel said, her mouth already full.

"And there's some French silk pie in the back when you're done with that."

She swallowed. "You're being really nice."

He shrugged and put the SUV in reverse. "I'm nice when you're nice to me."

It was a testament to how truly hungry Riel was that the sick feeling she got didn't stop her eating. She made herself smile at him. "Thank you."

"Don't mention it."

She bit into a piece of okra and wiped her hand on the back of her mouth. Her brow furrowed as she glanced around out the windows. "Where are we going?

"I have an open rental off of Burnside that you can stay in."

"I'm not staying at your house?"

He gave her a surprised look. "No, I didn't think Lizette should know about you being here. That might just complicate things."

A chill went down her spine that had nothing to do with the temperature. She should have known, but seeing Lizette had been the one thing she'd been looking forward to in all of this. She set her food aside and hugged her knees. Isaias snorted.

"You're not going to start playing me with the cold act again, are you? Come on, Riel."

"Please don't be mean about this, Isaias," she said quietly, gritting her teeth. "You know how I feel. Do you think it's easy for me?"

"Your sister is fine. She has her nice house and her kids. That's all she ever wanted, anyway. There's no passion in her at all. I thought there was, but it was just an act in the beginning."

"She's my sister."

"Like I said, you're doing her a favor. I've had something on the side most of the time, and it's never bugged her."

She fought back a powerful wave of anger, and kept herself from flinching away when Isaias pulled up to a stoplight and reached out to run his hand along her thigh. The effort caused beads of sweat to pop out on her neck, and she had another moment of panic, thinking she couldn't possibly keep it up. *This is too hard. I can't. I just can't. Not after what he's done.*

Then she took a deep breath and closed her eyes. She cleared her mind completely and became the act. Her life and her future depended on it. She slipped into an alternate skin, let herself feel feelings that weren't hers. Under the circumstances, it was a relief.

161

She opened her eyes again, blinking away tears. The light turned green and Isaias took his hand from her leg and turned onto Burnside. "That's not all that's bugging me about this," Riel said, her voice hoarse.

"What else?" he groaned. "What now?"

She clutched her elbows and stared out the side window at the damp sidewalks and storefronts. Daffodils were just starting to push their way out of the soil of the planters out front, cheerfully yellow in the watery sunlight. It was so much colder here than down south.

"It's just...Isaias, I've never been with a man before," she said. She glanced at him from the corner of her eye and felt a pang of triumph at his shell-shocked look.

"What, you're a virgin?" he said.

"I'm not a *virgin*, I've just never been with a *man* before."

Riel watched as that sank in. A fascinated smirk grew on his face. "You've fooled around with women, is what you're saying."

She focused her attention out the window, willing herself to not break character. "Yeah, I had a girlfriend in prison." She knew the FBI agents were listening to this conversation and wondered what they were thinking. Her earrings seemed suddenly heavy, and the phone in her pocket seemed to dig into her hip.

Isaias was silent for a moment. He pulled off into a narrow driveway between two three-story apartment buildings, and parked the SUV alongside an old Toyota covered in stickers. "You've really never had a cock in you? Shit, I don't believe that. What about Evan?" He cut the engine and looked at her.

Riel made her face blank and shrugged. "He wanted to, but he's a jerk, and I just don't like him that way." She met Isaias' eyes shyly. "It's always been you I wanted, even when I was little, when you and Lizette first got married." She dropped her gaze, her cheeks burning; it was from embarrassment at the depth of her lie, but he grinned wide and she knew she'd hit her mark.

"Let me show you what a man can do for you, Riel." He reached out and took her hand, stroking her fingers with his thumb. "I'll make you feel good in ways a woman never could."

"But Isaias, I…you know, I don't just want to be something else on the side for you. I want it to mean something. I want my first time with you to be something special."

He ran his fingers along her arm, her shoulder, brushed back her hair from her face. "You want the bed covered in rose petals or something? I can do that. Give me a minute to go to the store."

"No, Isaias." She brought her eyes to his. "I want it to be real. And I want to feel right about it."

Her heart hammered. If he got mad, her whole plan would fall apart right here. But his eyes were glazed over with lust, not anger. "What do you want, babe?" he asked.

"Once this deal goes through, you're going to have a buttload of money. I want you to set it up so that my sister and her kids are taken care of, otherwise I'm going to feel like total shit about this.

163

Then I want us to run off together, get set up somewhere else, somewhere warmer. You don't need Mama Maria anymore anyway. She's just taking all the money and not doing anything except boss you around. It's time for you to go it on your own."

She watched his eyes as he considered this. He made a face that was half scowl, half smile. "You're right about that, Riel."

She took his other hand, interlacing her fingers with his. "Will you do that for me? Just you and me, somewhere nice…and I can fuck you every night, and sleep in your arms."

His eyes shone, and he pulled her closer over the console, his hand sliding down to squeeze one of her breasts. "Partners in crime, huh?" he murmured in her ear. "That's not such a bad idea, Riel."

He kissed her, and she closed her eyes, imagining that it was Evan's lips on hers, his hand sliding up her shirt. She knew she had to give Isaias something in order to make this believable. She also knew he wouldn't give up trying to get her to go all the way. But, if all went as planned, in a few more days he'd be in jail and she wouldn't have to worry about his bullshit anymore.

Chapter Fifteen

The apartment Isaias set her up in wasn't so bad. It was furnished and had a view of the bustling street. But the cable and internet weren't working, there was no food in the kitchen, and she didn't have much to do but sit and wait. She wished she'd brought her guitar, but it had seemed like a bad idea. She might have to get out of here in a hurry, and then she'd have to leave it behind. But she wasn't really unhappy being alone in the quiet; at least she'd been able to get rid of Isaias.

She took a long nap and didn't wake up until after dark. She called Evan while she sat at the tiny dining table and munched on leftover fried chicken.

"I miss you so much," Evan said.

She smiled, twisting her hair between greasy fingers. "I miss you too. But it feels stupid talking about this over this line."

Evan laughed. "Hi, FBI agents! Should we have phone sex now?"

She snorted. "Probably better than most of the stuff they get to listen to."

The laughter drained out of his tone. "How is it going there, anyway? Is Isaias being a dickhole?"

"He's always a dickhole, but it's going okay. He's taking the bait so far. Tomorrow we're going to go meet the contact."

"He hasn't…you haven't…"

Riel closed her eyes, banishing the memory of Isaias' bad-tasting kiss. "No. I haven't."

Evan let out a breath. "Be careful. *Please*."

"I will." She pushed her limp coleslaw around the plate. "I just want this to be over with, so we can be together again."

"Me too," he said. "More than you know."

"Just a few more days."

"Yeah." He sighed. "I love you, Riel."

"I love you too."

***

Isaias picked her up at nine the next morning and took her to breakfast at a café down the street. He stared at her in fascination as she wolfed down bacon and roasted purple potatoes.

"How do you stay so skinny when you eat like that?" he asked.

She shrugged. "Genetics. My mom was skinny too."

A wave of sadness washed over her. Her mother had been a tiny woman with a gentle smile, but it would melt away in an instant, revealing the cold steel beneath. It had been so long since she'd died, and now all Riel had were fading photographs. She glanced up at Isaias, who was still watching her.

Mama would tell me to get this deal done, put this asshole in prison forever, and get on with leading an honest life. Lizette saved my life by marrying Isaias; now I can return the favor by getting rid of him.

She rolled her eyes. "Stop staring at me. I'm just hungry."

"It's sexy to watch you eat, that's all."

Her gaze fell to her plate, and she pushed her toast around, drawing patterns in the egg yolks.

"So tell me again about this guy we're meeting today," Isaias said, cutting up his ham. "You didn't tell me much on the phone."

"I didn't have time. I was worried Evan would walk in."

"I know, babe. But you're safe now." He reached over and pinched her thigh under the table.

Riel smashed a potato wedge under her fork. "This guy, name of La Percha, works for El Huracán directly, usually running to Mishmash. But when he found out I was your sister-in-law, he came and sounded me out. He says you already have a network down south, and maybe if you worked together you could cut Mishmash out of it."

"He'll want some of my cut, of course."

Riel shrugged. "But you'd be richer in the end, anyway, so I figured it'd be worth it."

"And this big deal you were talking about..."

They both went silent as the waitress approached, filling their coffee cups. Riel stirred some cream and sugar in hers as the woman wiggled off to the next table, Isaias' eyes following her round ass.

"There's a boat coming up off the coast north of Aberdeen," Riel continued in a low voice, and Isaias pulled his gaze back to hers. "It's a huge shipment of black tar that was supposed to be picked up by Mishmash himself, but La Percha says he can arrange for you to get it before Mishmash does."

Isaias laughed between bites of hash browns. "Leave him holding an empty bag. I love it." Then his smile faded and he gazed at her distantly, his brow furrowing as he cut another chunk off his ham steak.

"What?" Riel asked.

Isaias blinked and smiled. "Just thinking," he said, taking another bite of ham.

***

They crawled through traffic over the I-5 bridge to Vancouver, pulling off at a little strip mall restaurant that smelled of fish and garlic. They found La Percha in a back booth, wearing a John Deere hat like he'd said he would. He glanced up from his *sopa de mariscos*, smiling and wiping his moustache with a paper napkin as they scooted into the vinyl seat opposite him.

"*Buenas tardes,*" he said, shaking their hands. "You must be Isaias and Riel."

"Nice to make your acquaintance," Isaias said.

Percha and Riel exchanged the briefest of looks, a faint smile flitting across his lips before he focused all his attention on Isaias.

"Likewise," Percha said. "I've heard so much

about you, it's nice to put a face to all the *chisme*."
He grinned and spooned up some more soup. "So,
we can work together, *que no*?"

"Maybe we could," Isaias said, leaning back in
his seat and crossing his arms. "Sounds like we
could make a little pile off of this shipment, and
then each of us could come out a little ahead on
other business."

Percha nodded, his eyes flicking over to the
waiter, who approached them, smiling solicitously
at Isaias and Riel.

"*Buenas tardes.* Can I get you two anything?"

Riel ordered a Coke, and Isaias got a plate of
ceviche, even though they'd eaten only an hour
before. When the man left, Isaias ran his hand over
his hair, mussing it on purpose so that it stood up
rakishly. Riel watched him, struck by the fact that
he was a full ten years older than her sister, crow's
feet beginning to show around his eyes. He was still
playing the part of the cocky young punk, still
trying to get out from under his mother's heavy
thumb, and trying to be a man and a boy at the same
time. He was failing on all counts.

"My biggest problem with this," Isaias said, "is
that Mishmash is going to retaliate hard when he
figures out who's engineered this *chingadera*. No
part of this plan actually gets him out of the
picture."

Percha shrugged, spooning up a chunk of fish.
"We cut him out of it, he's bound to get mad. But
up here he hasn't got many people. We can take
care of him later when our network is stronger." He
slurped his soup.

"Why wait?" Isaias said. "He'll be up here himself for this deal, so why not *matar a dos pájaros de un tiro*?"

Percha and Isaias regarded each other over the cluttered table as Riel clenched her teeth against her panic. She didn't like the emphasis that Isaias had put on *matar,* "kill." Percha's gaze darted to hers for a brief second, then away again, locking once more on Isaias. Riel thought she knew what that glance meant. She pulled her phone out of her pocket and pretended to play with it, not wanting the microphone to miss any part of this conversation.

"You want us to do a hit on Mishmash ourselves?" Percha said. "Because, to me, getting away clean with the dope sounds like the most lucrative option."

"Us three will get away with the dope. I'll arrange for the hit," Isaias replied.

Percha folded his hands on the table. "Your guys are going to figure out there's a big shipment involved and demand heavier payment than they would otherwise."

"My guys will do what I tell them. I'm not worried about that."

Percha's gaze hardened as he studied Isaias' face. "So you're only telling me this because you want part of their payment to come out of my cut."

"Seems fair."

"Not when I don't agree. Much safer to deal with Mishmash later, when we're well out of it."

"And give him time to get organized and hit back? Doesn't make much sense."

Percha squinted at him, tapping his thumbs against the veneer tabletop as the waiter brought Riel's Coke. She stirred her straw around as the waiter left again, rolling her neck around to loosen her muscles. Percha nodded slightly. "Okay, but I'm only paying an eighth of their take on the deal. *Y no me jodes* by saying it costs more than it does, because I know what it should cost."

"I'm not going to fuck you over. If we're going to work together, the first thing you have to learn about me is that I'm fair. I do business, sure, and I take what's mine, but I don't screw an honest man out of his money. Now do me the same favor by paying half."

"This is your game," Percha insisted. "I'm just a lowly runner. I don't stand to make half the profits, so why should I pay half the costs?"

"If you're a lowly runner then I'm a fucking *chango*. I'm helping you to get a leg up, and you stand to make some good money, better than you'd make with Mishmash."

"Yeah, but not *half*. You gonna pay me half your profits on this, *señor chango*?"

Riel tensed as the two men glared at each other across the table, Percha smiling tightly.

"I'll pay you three percent over what Mishmash was paying you," Isaias said, "which is more than fair considering you'll pick up more work if he's out of it." Riel relaxed slightly.

"Make it ten over what he pays me, and I pay fifteen percent of the hit," Percha replied. "That's more than fair."

They continued to haggle, pausing only when the

171

waiter came to serve the *ceviche*. Riel watched Percha closely while pretending to look at her phone. He was playing his part almost too convincingly, and she got a jolt of fear wondering if he wasn't some sort of double agent, or if he didn't have some other angle on this. Her stomach cramped. What if Mishmash ended up really getting killed because of her?

But the agents were listening in. They wouldn't let that happen, right?

Eventually they came to terms, Percha agreeing to pay twenty percent of the cost of the hit. They shook hands over the table, and Percha paid the check. They stood up to leave, and Riel shoved the phone into her back pocket.

"It's very nice to meet you guys," Percha said with a faint smile at Riel. "I know this is going to be a productive relationship."

Riel returned his smile, wiping the sweat from the back of her neck.

"I'm sure it'll be a long and happy marriage," Isaias said.

Chapter Sixteen

Isaias backed her up against the wall of the apartment, holding her there with his wet lips and overly-enthusiastic tongue. He grabbed her tits and squeezed them like gigantic stress balls, his disappointing hard-on smashed against her belly. Riel wrapped her arms around him, returning his kiss, feeling like she was standing outside her body, like a film director.

His hand worked its way down under the waistband of her jeans, and she struggled gently away.

"Isaias…"

"Ah, babe, you're so beautiful," he murmured, sliding his fingers down further and stroking her clit roughly. "Let me bury my cock up in that sweet pussy. I promise I'll be gentle, and I'll make you come so hard, Rielita."

She had to pry her lips from his again. "Just wait, Isaias. It will be better…it will be so good if we wait."

He groaned, pressing his wet lips to her neck. "I

need you so bad right now."

She swallowed the bile creeping up her throat. "I'd feel horrible afterwards. I just want this to be right. It's something I'll remember for the rest of my life, and I don't want anything to ruin it. It's only a couple more days…"

He sighed and took his hands off of her. He leaned back against the wall on his clenched fists, his eyes closed and his face pale. Riel stood, tense, waiting.

He straightened. "You're killing me," he said. Then a wry smile twisted his mouth, and Riel flattened herself against the wall, her heart beating fast. But he didn't reach for her again; he shoved off and headed for the door. "I'll see you tomorrow, babe."

Riel's shoulders slumped with relief as the door closed behind him, and she threw herself on the couch, clutching her head in her hands. This was just an act. It wasn't even really happening to *her*. This was an alternate Riel, one that existed only to get this job done. Once Isaias was in prison, the fake Riel would disappear, and the memory of Isaias' ungentle hands and disgusting lips would disappear along with her. She only hoped she'd make it to that day alive and intact.

Riel twitched as her phone buzzed in her back pocket. She pulled it out.

It was a text from a blocked number:

Unknown: **Meet the woman with red hair and green denim jacket at the Hot Box Café at 4:30 p.m. Delete this after reading.**

Riel deleted the text and checked the time, her heart pounding in her ears. It was 3:45. She'd seen the Hot Box further down Burnside as they'd driven past; it was probably a five minute walk.

She wondered what the feds had to say to her. It couldn't be good: she didn't remember them saying anything about a meeting, so something must have gone wrong. What could it be? Was the mission in danger?

She got up and paced the apartment, opening cupboards, finding a bottle of spray cleaner and shriveled sponge, wiping down the already clean kitchen counters. She touched up her makeup, brushed her hair, and then stared at her phone for the last five minutes until it was time to leave.

The damp evening air had formed a dew on her cheeks by the time she shouldered her way through the café door, setting off a string of dangling prayer bells. The air was stuffy with the smell of sandalwood and damp wool hats. Kishi Bashi played on the stereo system.

Riel spotted the red-haired woman in the green jacket at a dimly-lit booth in the back. Their eyes met, and the woman smiled and waved. Riel wove through the tables to slide into the booth across from her.

"Hi, Riel," the woman said. "I'm Catherine."

Riel smiled, twisting her fingers together under the table. "Hi, Catherine." The agent had on a lot of eye makeup, and her beauty was marred somewhat by a heavy jaw. It was hard to tell her age; she was dressed like a young hipster, but something in her glance and the way she held herself told Riel she was older, probably in her thirties.

A waiter approached, his thin face etched with geometric tattoos. Riel glanced down at her menu, her stomach feeling sick. They didn't have Coke, and she didn't feel like coffee. She settled on a pomegranate soda, and Catherine ordered a basket of taro fries and a kava chocolate milkshake.

When the waiter was gone, Catherine glanced around. "How are you holding up?"

Riel shrugged stiffly. "I'll be glad when this is over, that's all."

Catherine gave her a knowing look. "Listen, this job is getting rough for you, and it's getting complicated all around, so we wanted to let you know that there's a way out, if you want it. We have a recording of Isaias planning a hit against Mishmash, and planning to retrieve a shipment of drugs. That, along with the circumstantial evidence we already have, might be enough to prove conspiracy and racketeering charges against him, so if you want to bug out now, you could."

Riel's heart pounded in her hollow chest. She could forget about this. She could go back to Evan right now and start a new life. But something in Catherine's gaze brought the heaviness rushing back to settle over her shoulders.

"You *might* be able to prove conspiracy and racketeering charges. What are the chances you couldn't?"

The woman's thin lips twitched in a slight grimace. "Not even a lawyer would give you odds, and I'm not a lawyer. But I will tell you the case isn't nearly as strong as we'd like it to be. The recording we have might be enough to send him away for a bit, but in absence of other hard evidence, a good lawyer could say it was all bluster, or a joke, or even entrapment. Assuming we did get a conviction, the sentence wouldn't likely be very long. A few years at most."

Riel chewed her lip. "If we go all the way through with this, the chances of him going to prison for a long time would be better?"

Catherine nodded. "When he actually has the drugs in his possession, and the hit men are poised to act, it should be fairly easy to get a conviction. If we have those two elements together—the hit and the drug deal—we can get a conviction under the federal racketeering statute, and it will also be easier to prove more counts against him with the circumstantial evidence we have, and put him away for a long time. That's what we were aiming for originally…but the risks are pretty high for you right now."

Riel wrinkled her nose at the look Catherine was giving her. "I can handle it."

"It's a dangerous game you're playing," the agent said. "I know you're just doing what you have to do, but Isaias could get violent if you don't give him what he wants. It could blow the whole mission if we have to come in to save you before the deal is complete."

Riel stared down at the table, the conversation and music in the restaurant swimming around her ears. She looked up, a bit startled, when the waiter came back with the fries and drinks. He gave her a cute smile that changed the pattern of his tattoos, his brown eyes lingering on hers. "Can I get you anything else?"

A different life. She smiled back. "No, I think we're good."

He left, and Riel looked back up at Catherine. "I came back up here to make sure Isaias goes to prison for a long time, and I'm going to see that through. If I give up now, I won't get another chance, and if I don't take it I'd never be able to forgive myself. If he's acquitted or gets a short sentence, he'll hurt me, and my sister, and Evan."

"We'd do all we can to prevent that," Catherine said.

Riel shook her head. "I wouldn't be able to sleep at night, knowing it was possible he'd find one of us."

Catherine regarded her a long while, then nodded slightly. "I understand." Then she leaned over the table, fiddling with her napkin. "There's something else. This is off the record, and technically I shouldn't be saying this, but…you wanted him to set it up so your sister and her kids would be taken care of after all this is over…"

Riel tensed. "What's the problem?"

"Well, once we bring charges, we'll seize all his assets. That would include anything in his wife's name or under the names of any of his companies. His mother will face charges with him, so anything in her name wouldn't be safe, either. I'm not sure there's any way around that."

Riel swallowed, and pressed the heels of her hands into her eyes. "So Lizette will be bankrupt. She'll have nothing. She'll still be rid of that

fucktard, but I'm not sure she'll really thank me for
it."

"There are other ways."

Riel put her hands down. "How?"

"Get him to put the money in someone else's
name, someone not connected with this stuff at all.
Then, when legal gets a hold of this case, we'll have
an easier time keeping that money from being
seized. You'll just have to make sure your sister
doesn't use it to hire him a lawyer or help him any
other way, because they'll figure it out quick in that
case."

She thought of her sister, pale and miserable,
stuck in a horrible marriage. But still, she loved
Isaias. Would she try to help him after he was
arrested? She clenched her hands into fists. "I'll
make sure she won't," Riel said.

Catherine nodded, smiling warmly.

*The real problem would be convincing Isaias to
put the money in someone else's name.* He'd be
suspicious that she was up to something, afraid
she'd run off, that she was playing him. And whose
name would the money be connected to, anyway?
Someone not connected with this, but who wouldn't
take the money and run themselves. She chewed her
cheek so hard she tasted blood, while Catherine
picked up a handful of fries, fixing her with a stare
that Riel might have called motherly, if she could
remember what a motherly stare looked like.

"Listen," the agent said. "You're brave, and
smart, and tough, and you've got the U.S.
Government on your side. We're going to figure
this out, okay?"

Riel nodded. "Yeah. We'll figure it out. Thanks."

***

Riel tossed around, tangling herself up in the scratchy blankets. The streetlights leaked through the curtains and stained the ceiling a watery orange, throwing every bead of the popcorn ceiling into high relief. Riel had memorized every pattern in that ceiling, the slack-jawed faces, weirdly-shaped animals, and misspelled words hidden in the smattering of dots. Her brain felt like dry toast. The alarm clock shone a dull red, turning over the minutes one by one. It was two fourteen in the morning.

All the potential conversations she could have with Isaias to convince him to give her the money for her sister rolled through her mind, each of them fragmenting toward the end as they broke down under the pressure of logic. There was no explanation she could give him for the request that wouldn't invite dangerous questions.

She tossed over again. She wasn't even getting any new ideas at this point. Her brain was stuck in a loop, wandering down the same well-worn pathways. *If only there were some way to transfer the money from Lizette's name to another without him knowing.*

The relentless march of minutes dragged toward dawn, grey light dimming the streetlamp's glare, before she sat up, flinging off the blankets. There was only one way she could think of. It was dangerous, but she'd have to try something.

180

The clock said six twenty-two. She grabbed her phone from the bedside table, hesitating. Her sister would probably be up now, Isaias still sleeping.

But what if she wasn't up? What if Lizette answered the phone still in bed, a groggy Isaias right next to her?

And what if she told her husband that Riel had called her? Did she really love him? Would she be loyal, or was she just sticking around because she had nowhere else to go?

When they'd been girls, Riel and Lizette had been very close. Their parents were gone a lot, always working, and it was just the two of them together, taking care of each other, watching out for each other. Then, when their parents had died, they'd really only had one another. It had been them against the world.

Until Isaias came into the picture. Lizette had latched onto him like a life raft. He was their ticket out of the horrible poverty that threatened to claim them, the hunger and uncertainty that gnawed at them every night, the worry that the government would come and put Riel, or both of them, in foster homes. The stability that Isaias offered had made Lizette idolize him, and had quickly turned into a fierce love and devotion. That love had apparently soured somewhat over the years as Isaias showed his true nature, but was it still strong enough that Lizette would choose him over her own sister?

And then there was the FBI, listening in on the conversation. Would they go along with this, even though they'd easily be able to follow the trail of money? Or would they double-cross her and her sister once this deal was through, and seize the assets anyway?

There were so many other risks, so many things that could go wrong. Riel tugged her fingers through her disheveled hair. There was no point agonizing. It was her only hope. She dialed her sister's number.

Her heart beat painfully as it rang, and Riel sent up a silent prayer that Lizette was alone. That she'd be sitting in the kitchen with her coffee, enjoying the only quiet moment of her day before everyone else was up.

It rang once, twice, a third time, and Riel balled the sheets up in her sweaty fists. Midway through the fourth ring, there was a click, and a quiet, uncertain voice came on the line. "Hello?"

"Lizette?"

There was a short silence, in which Riel's muscles tightened like bowstrings. "Riel, is that you?"

"Yes. Is Isaias with you right now?"

"No, he's in bed. Oh my God, Riel, where are you?"

"I'm back here in Portland. Be quiet, Lizette, don't let Isaias hear that I'm talking to you, okay?"

She lowered her voice. "What happened? He said you ran away with that Evan."

"I did for a little while, but I'm back." Riel took a deep breath. "Listen, Lizette. If I talk to you about something, can you promise you won't tell Isaias?"

Lizette's voice shook slightly. "What is it, Riel? What's going on?"

"You have to promise me you won't tell him,

that you won't say anything to *anybody*. Because if you tell, it could put us in danger, all of us. You, me, Isaias, the kids. Can you promise?"

There was another silence, and Riel squeezed the sheets so hard her hand started to ache. "I promise," Lizette finally said. "I won't say anything."

Riel let out the breath she'd been holding. "Good. Good. Okay, Lizette...pretty soon, hopefully, Isaias is going to give you a bunch of money, put it in an account for you."

"What? Why?"

"I don't know what he'll tell you it's for, but the real reason is we're doing something risky, and he wants to make sure you and the kids are taken care of in case something happens."

"Riel, what are you doing? Don't, whatever it is, just don't do it if it's too dangerous—"

"We have to do it. And don't worry, we'll be okay. This is all just in case."

"But, Riel—"

"I'll explain it all so that you'll understand afterwards. Please, just trust me."

Lizette sobbed into the phone. "I hate this so much. I hate that you guys do this work. I wish..."

She broke down, and Riel's lips tightened. "You wish you'd hadn't been pulled into this crap. You wish Isaias made his money some other way...or that you hadn't married him at all." Lizette sobbed again in response, and Riel listened, hoping the latter was the correct explanation, that Lizette wished she was rid of her horrible husband. "Well, you knew what his work was when you married him, Lizette. You knew what you were getting

183

into."

"Riel—"

"And besides, that's why we're doing this," Riel cut in. "To escape this business. If this works out, you won't have to worry anymore."

"What do you mean?"

"No more mob bullshit, Lizette. We can all live normal lives."

Lizette sniffed and took a shuddering breath. "Really?"

"Really."

Her sister's voice steadied. "What do I have to do?"

Riel squeezed her eyes shut. "There's a United Bank account under the name of Nora Mejia. I'll text you the account and routing numbers. Put the money in there. And if something happens to me—"

"Riel, if something happens to you, I'm not going to be worried about money—"

"I'm going to be fine, everything's going to be okay, but *just in case,* Lizette. Because if something happens, you and the kids are still going to need money. I just can't rest easy unless I know you guys are going to be okay, no matter what."

Lizette began to cry again, not saying anything.

"I'm going to text you a number," Riel continued. "If something happens to me, call it. This person will send you the documents you need in order to access the money yourself. I'm going to be fine, everything is going to work out, and I'll be able to get the money back to you in person, but just in case, okay?"

"Okay, Riel," Lizette said quietly. "But, please,

just be really careful. You shouldn't be doing this at all. You should just run away."

Riel couldn't keep herself from snorting. "Where would I go, that they wouldn't find me? If it's so easy, why don't *you* run away?"

Riel waited breathlessly for her sister's answer.

"I have the kids," Lizette finally said, her voice shaking. "I need to take care of them. And Isaias…he's my husband…"

"I know he's your husband," Riel said bitterly. "But he's a *cabrón*, Lizette."

The pressure on Riel's heart eased when Lizette gave a watery laugh. That laugh died quickly into silence, however, and she spoke with a note of desperation in her voice. "I know he's not perfect," Lizette said, "but he takes care of us."

Riel clutched the phone. "And if you could take care of yourself and the kids without him? Would you do it?"

Riel's pounding heart rang into the silence. Lizette couldn't be loyal to that asshole, she just couldn't.

Lizette sniffed. "Yes," she finally said, her voice barely audible. "If I could get out of this life, I would."

Riel let out a breath. *Thank God.* "We're going to get through this, Lizette."

"I know we will. Just be careful."

"You too, Lizette. I love you."

"I love you too, Gabrielita."

Riel hung up the phone and collapsed into bed. She'd done all she could. Now it was up to Isaias, her sister, and the FBI to keep their promises.

Chapter Seventeen

Riel was jolted out of a confused dream where she was searching for someplace to hide a bowling ball full of money. Consciousness surprised her, and she gasped and flailed, tangling herself up in blankets.

A hand reached out and grabbed her waist. "It's okay, babe. Shhhh."

She got a rush of adrenaline, but she made herself stop struggling. "Isaias?"

He pulled her closer. "Yeah, Rielita, don't worry, it's me. Why are you still in bed?"

"I couldn't sleep last night. What time is it?"

"Nine thirty."

Riel groaned, closing her sandy eyes. "I'm so tired. I didn't get to sleep until late."

He scooted closer, stretching out beside her and stroking her back. "Oh? Why not?"

"I just can't stop worrying about this deal going wrong. I keep playing it over and over in my mind." She looked up at him through her eyelashes. "Why do you have to complicate it by calling a hit on

186

Mishmash right now? Percha was right, it'd be better to wait, after we're away with the money."

"We won't be safe with Mishmash out there, and I won't be able to take over his route as easily."

"If you kill him, how do you know his people won't retaliate even harder than Mishmash would have, if he were still alive? It's one thing to screw him over, another to kill him. He has loyal men, Isaias. And how do you know that the bigger guys won't get pissed and call a hit on us for messing with their business like that?"

He stroked her hair back from her forehead. "Mishmash is small potatoes. No one is going to lose sleep over him being taken out."

"I'm not sure that's true. Even if his people don't retaliate out of loyalty, they'll do it just because they want to take over his piece for themselves. And the bosses don't like it when people on this level get too big."

He kissed her lightly. "You worry too much, little girl."

Riel clamped her jaw down in frustration, her gaze darting to her phone sitting on the bedside table. She hoped they were hearing all of this clearly, and that they could stop Mishmash from getting hurt.

She made herself relax as his hand slid down to her ass and squeezed. He pressed his body against hers. "Ah, babe, stop worrying."

"I can't, Isaias."

He dragged his fingers around the curve of her hip, up between her legs. "I know something that will relax you."

"Isaias—"

"Let me slide it up between those beautiful thighs and fuck you so good, Riel. Please."

Riel closed her eyes and let go of herself, banishing her ego and clearing her head. *This isn't the real Riel. This is all pretend.* "Yeah?" she murmured. "You give Lizette her money yet?"

"I will," he said, fondling her tits. "Today."

"You promise? I need to feel right about this, Isaias."

"I promise." He kissed her, pulling her tight against him, his cock throbbing against her leg. "Tell me what your girlfriend did to you to make you come," he muttered in her ear. "What was her name? Your girlfriend in prison."

"Marissa," she said. Riel remembered the feel of Marissa's firm, silky tits and felt a pang of arousal. She clung to it, her mental life raft.

"Marissa," Isaias breathed. "Tell me about her."

"She had this amazing, dark skin, and an amazing ass. I loved the way it felt in my hands, all round and firm but still soft."

He kissed her neck, his hands everywhere, but she hardly felt it, consumed by her fantasy. "Yeah?" Isaias said. "What kind of things did you do to each other, Riel?"

"My favorite thing was when one of the good guards would give us bathroom cleaning duty together, so we'd have some time. We'd get into one of the showers completely naked and turn the warm water on." Riel ached. She felt herself get wet, remembering. "She'd suck on my nipples, and put her fingers inside me. Then she'd kiss my body, put her lips everywhere, soft kisses that felt good and tingly, and then she'd bite me just a little bit sometimes."

Riel drew a breath as the fantasy filled her head, Isaias disappearing completely from her world. "She'd get on her knees and rub my clit with her little tongue." Riel slid her hand down her pajama bottoms and rubbed, imagining Marissa's wet, sensitive tongue there. "She was so good with her tongue, and she'd push her fingers in me real slow and deep, how I liked it, and she knew right where it felt good." Riel rubbed slow and hard, her hips pressing up against her hand, and slipped two fingers deep inside her wet pussy, moaning softly. "She fucked me slow like that, until I wanted it, I wanted it hard, I'd be begging her until she finally banged me, fucked me hard up against the shower tile. She'd make me come..." Riel gasped as waves of pleasure broke over her, a small cry escaping her lips.

She came back slowly to reality. Isaias was squeezing her ass and stroking his cock; he grunted and gasped, then pulled his hand from his pants.

Riel blinked, laying stiffly as he kissed her.

"Ah, babe, I can't wait until tomorrow night, when this deal is taken care of, and we can get away," he said.

Riel squeezed her eyes shut. "Me neither," she said.

***

Isaias waited while she took a long shower, then

he took her out to breakfast. She sat poking at her crepes with her fork while he chomped down his breakfast *fajitas*.

"What story are you going to tell Lizette about why you're giving her the money?" Riel asked. "Isn't she going to get suspicious?"

Isaias shrugged, swallowing. "She knows not to ask too many questions. I'll just tell her I need to spread the cash out a bit so I don't have too much in one place."

She made herself meet his gaze. "How much are you going to give her?"

He grinned lopsidedly, taking another bite of *fajita*. He spoke with his mouth full, Riel dodging the crumbs he launched at her. "Worried about your own prospects when you're with me? Don't worry, Rielita, I won't give her all of it."

Riel unclenched her teeth. "It's not that. I know you'll take care of us. I just need to know Lizette and the kids are taken care of too. Lizette's had a hard life, Isaias. She made sure I had a good home through it all. She's done so much for me."

He put the *fajita* down and reached over to pat her hand, leaving dabs of steak grease on her skin. "I'll make sure she and the kids have enough. And they have the house, which is all paid for. They'll do fine."

Riel forced a smile, her cheeks aching. Would the feds take the house too? She didn't know. "You're such a good man, Isaias," she said.

"I try to be," he said, grinning.

***

Isaias dropped her back at the apartment, telling her he had to take care of a few things, and so Riel was left to wander through the drab rooms, chewing her lip. Eventually she went out and sat in a coffee shop, thinking it would be easier to wrestle her agitation if she were surrounded by distraction. She sat on a stool by the window and watched people strolling over damp sidewalks sheened with oil, walking their dogs, laughing with each other. They existed in a different world than she did. A cleaner, more organized world. She felt like she was free-falling, gazing enviously at the people standing on solid ground, and wondered, as she had so many times before, what it would have been like to grow up in a safe home with loving parents. To be one of these happy people with a "normal" life. To not have to worry about her next meal, or going to jail, or getting shot.

She clutched her coffee mug, her short fingernails bending against the smooth porcelain. It was no use railing against life's unfairness. She had to do the best she could with what she had, so that maybe, someday, she could be one of those carefree people with a house, a loving family, and a cat.

As evening began to fall, clouds billowing in over the rosy sunset, Riel tromped back to the apartment. She sat with her back against the wall of the bedroom and called Evan.

"I told Lizette to call you if something happens to me, so that you can send her fake documents in the name of Nora Mejia," Riel said, picking at the carpet. "That way she'll be able to access the money herself. I know you'll help her change the info on

191

there, you know, put her picture."

Evan huffed so loudly that it hurt Riel's ear. "That's too dangerous, you calling her and telling her that, Riel. What if Isaias figures this out?"

"He won't," Riel said. "Lizette won't tell him."

"Yeah, but if he's watching her closely, keeping tabs on her phone calls and texts…"

"I don't think he'd do that. He doesn't even respect her enough to think she'd double-cross him, you know? He's an idiot."

"Isaias isn't really an idiot. He's not the most observant, but he's not dumb. I think you have the wrong impression because of the way he acts around you."

"Whatever. He's an idiot."

Evan sighed heavily. "Jesus, Riel, this thing is just…I can't stand it. It just seems too messy, and I have a bad feeling."

"Don't worry," she said. "This time tomorrow, it'll all be over, and we'll be home free."

There was a short silence, and she thought she heard him sniffing. "I hope you're right," he said.

I hope I am too. "I *am* right," she said. "You'll see."

After she hung up, she sat there, staring blankly at the wall, aching everywhere from the constant tension in her muscles. She was exhausted, but didn't feel like she could sleep. There were too many questions, too many worries.

Riel was anxious. Everything could go wrong tomorrow. The FBI might not be able to stop the hit on Mishmash. She could end up hurt, or worse. The feds could renege on their deal, and she'd end up back in prison.

But strangely enough, her biggest worry was that Isaias wouldn't actually give Lizette any money. He could easily lie about it, and then she wouldn't be able to do anything until it was too late. She sat tapping the screen of her phone, itching to call her sister.

She checked the time. Eight forty-two. Usually by this time Isaias had eaten dinner and gone out for the evening. Would it be safe to call?

Riel cursed. She knew she'd never sleep if she didn't. Forcing her heart out of her throat, she picked up her phone and dialed.

Lizette answered on the second ring. "Riel?"

"Is Isaias gone?"

"Yeah, he's out."

Riel let out a breath. "Thank God. I just wanted to make sure he'd talked to you about the money."

There was an excited note in Lizette's voice. "He did. I actually saw the account balance sheets. He gave me almost two million dollars, Riel."

Riel laughed. "Oh, my God. That's so good."

Lizette gave a nervous giggle. "Yeah, I never really knew how much money he has. It must be a lot. I'm going to do what you said, first thing tomorrow, and transfer it to that account."

"Good. It'll be safe there, and after this is all over, I'll transfer it back to you." Riel would have to figure out how that could work without getting the feds involved, but there would be plenty of time for that after Isaias was in prison. "Lizette, thank you for everything you've done for me," Riel said. "You know, keeping me safe after Dad and Mama died. I know it wasn't easy for you."

"You're my sister. I'd do anything for you. And it hasn't exactly been easy for you, either."

"You didn't know things would turn out the way they did," Riel said, her mouth suddenly sour. "And it could have ended up a lot worse if we'd been on the streets or I'd ended up in foster care. You did a good job, Lizzy. You took care of us."

Lizette's voice shook. "I feel horrible about it, you know, how Isaias treated you. I always have. I tried to tell him to leave you out of it, but you know how he and Mama Maria can get. I just felt like…"

"Yeah, I know," Riel said.

They were silent for a moment, and Riel felt the old camaraderie growing between them, like it had been in the old days. Just them, together, against the world. "I love you, Lizzy," she said.

"I love you too, *hermanita.*"

Riel hung up, then crawled into bed, finally feeling drowsy. *Whatever happens, at least Lizette and the kids are taken care of. The rest of it, I can't control. I'll just have to deal with it as it happens.*

She hugged her pillow and fell asleep.

***

Riel came awake with a start when she heard the door to the apartment open. Adrenaline brought her up out of bed before Isaias could crawl in with her.

He strode into the room as she pulled a sweatshirt on over her pajamas. He was smiling, but something about his look made Riel freeze.

"Good morning, Rielita," he said. "You sleep

good?"

"Yeah," she said, watching him. "Much better than the night before."

"*Bueno.*" She stood rigid as he came over to her and put an arm around her waist. What was it about him that was putting her on edge? He kissed her, and she relaxed slightly. She must be imagining it, or maybe it was just nerves about this deal today.

His hand found its way underneath her clothes, squeezing a breast. He stepped forward, slowly pushing her back, his kisses hungry, and his hands slow and insistent. She jumped slightly as she felt her ass unexpectedly touch the wall. He pressed her against it with his body.

"Ah, Rielita," he murmured. "You're so hot."

"You are too, Isaias."

He laughed softly. Then, in a quick movement, he brought his forearm up against her throat, slamming her back.

He gave her a clenched-teeth grin. "You're so hot, you're gonna burn in hell, you fucking cunt."

Chapter Eighteen

For a moment, Riel was too shocked even to struggle. She stared up into Isaias' vicious eyes, trying to get a breath with his arm barred across her throat. He smiled a tight smile and slammed her against the wall again. Lights flashed in her skull.

"You think you can fuck with me, Riel?"

"Isaias, what—" she wheezed, but he cut her off.

"I saw you'd called Lizette, so she and I had a little chat. Thought you could fuck me out of that money, fuck over your poor sister, and run off? I know Nora Mejia is your fake ID. I figured it out after those *pinche bobosos* at the border let you go. I know that you wanted that money transferred to you."

Riel's ears rang with panic. She tried to shake her head, her chin twitching back and forth as it hung on his arm. Her mind was racing too quickly for coherent thought; the only thing she could think to do was deny it. He pressed his arm tighter against her throat, and darkness began to close in.

"Don't play me, you cunt," he said. Then he took

196

his arm from her throat and grasped her wrist roughly, pulling her toward the door so hard her joints popped. "You still with Evan? Or is it Mishmash that's getting a cut of this deal? Is that why you were all, 'Oooh, Isaias, don't kill him'?"

She opened her mouth to respond, to say something, anything, but he cut her off again.

"Don't bother. You'll have plenty of time to tell me the story later." He grinned and shoved her against the door, his lips and furious eyes inches from hers. "Thank your lucky stars you're so fuckable, or I'd just kill you now. But I'm still going to get a good bang or two out of you, Rielita. What happens to you afterwards depends on how good you are."

He opened the door and pulled her out, his grip on her wrist so tight her hand tingled. She stumbled after him down the stairwell, the nonskid surface scraping her bare feet.

Her breath wheezed in her sore, tight throat, and sweat ran down the back of her neck. With a jolt, she realized she'd left her phone back on the bedside table, along with the earrings, which she'd taken out before going to sleep.

She cursed inwardly. Would they be able to convict him without a recording?

Right now, just worry about getting out of this alive.

A shiny blue Impala was idling out front. As Isaias shoved her in the backseat, another thought occurred to her that made her weak: what if Isaias had stopped Lizette before she could transfer the money? *And what did he do to my sister? He*

197

wouldn't punish her for something I did, would he?

Then she realized that the FBI would have heard him threatening her in the bedroom before they left, and she closed her eyes, taking a deep breath. Would they abort the mission and come arrest him before the drug deal was done, and ruin the chances of a good sentence?

Or what if they can't come at all? What if something happens, and I get stuck with him?

She shoved the thoughts away. She had to keep her head clear. She had to think of something, play her part.

They pulled away from the curb. The driver was a guy with shoulders twice as wide as his seat, a sleek, black ponytail hanging down his back. His brown eyes flicked to the rearview to examine her with mild curiosity.

"Don't bother trying to escape, Riel," Isaias said. "The child locks are on, and we'll fucking cap you if you make a move. I can get a piece of ass elsewhere if you cause me any trouble."

"Isaias," Riel said, her hands tightening on her knees, "I'm not going to try to escape. And I wasn't going to run off with the money."

"Fucking save your shit, bitch. I don't know exactly what your game is, whether you're working alone or with someone, but I know you've been scamming me."

"I'm not lying. I never planned on taking the money from Lizette. I didn't tell you that I'd talked to Lizette because I knew you'd think that I was pulling some hustle, but I was worried, you know, if something happens…if we get shot…the police are going to know it's gang related, right? And don't they take all your assets if they suspect you of gang activity? That's what they told me in prison. And they take the other person's assets and property too, if you're married, so that would include anything in Lizette's name. I just wanted her to be safe, Isaias. You know that. She's my *sister*." A lump rose in her throat, tears pouring down her cheeks. "You didn't...you didn't hurt her, right? She didn't do anything—"

"She got what she deserved," Isaias said. "And save your stories, Rielita. I've got better things to think about besides your bullshit right now."

Riel hugged herself tightly, trying to control her sobs. "What did you do to her?"

"Don't worry about it. It's none of your fucking business."

She gritted her teeth. "It wasn't her fault, it was me. And I wasn't doing anything wrong, anyway. Please believe me, Isaias. I'd never hurt you or Lizette. I just...just in case..."

He looked back at her, his expression making her stomach drop. "Just in case we got busted? Why are you so worried about that, Rielita? You gonna snitch us off too?"

Her heart skipped a beat. "No, I'd never—"

Isaias reached back and shoved her hard into the car door. She cried out, bringing her hands up in front of her face. The car swerved slightly. "Take it easy, man," the driver said.

"Just shut up, both of you," Isaias said. "I don't want to listen to you right now, Riel. You fucked this shit all up and I had to work all night to get the location of the pickup and the hit moved, in case you'd tipped Mishmash off. You're lucky I don't beat you six feet underground right now, you fucking *puta*."

Riel curled around her knees, this new piece of information sinking in like a knife. Would the police know about the new plans? She didn't know if they had ways of spying on him other than her phone.

They wound through the city, taking a small highway toward the coast. The bare branches of the trees were just starting to show a green fuzz of new leaves, and the sun shone, the blue sky contrasting with the bright silver of the broken, puffy clouds. It was such a beautiful day, and Riel's heart ached, wondering if she'd survive to see another. She wondered if her sister were still alive to see this one.

The congestion of the city thinned out, the overpasses and buildings giving way to mixed forests and farms. Riel expected to hear sirens, for police to surround them, but all remained quiet. Had they decided not to abort the mission, or did law enforcement just not know where they were? The GPS tracker was back in the apartment, and they were going south instead of north, as they'd originally planned.

Isaias put music on, and he and the driver, who he called Marty, chatted idly about different bands. Riel concentrated on keeping herself under control, trying not to worry about what was going on with the cops and with Lizette.

The farms grew few and far between, the trees

became more numerous. Isaias' and Marty's conversation moved to some show that was on HBO. They seemed to have forgotten she was there, which was fine with her.

The highway cut west between wide meadows, then started climbing the Coast Range, the sun dappling the highway between the tall branches of pines and broadleaf maples. Riel's foot was jittering, her mouth dry. She couldn't stay silent any longer.

"Isaias," she said. "What are you going to do with me?"

Marty's eyes briefly found hers in the rearview. He looked mildly amused, and she pushed back her anger.

"You and I are going away, just like we planned," Isaias said. "What happens to you after that depends on a lot of things, like how good you fuck me, and how much someone else will pay for a backstabbing slut like you when I'm done. I'm guessing you'll probably end up dead." He laughed, and Riel felt sick.

They drove back down out of the hills, and took a winding back road through farms, their forgotten outbuildings half-hidden by tangles of blackberry vines. They topped a rise, and the sweep of the blue-grey Pacific came into view, making Riel's heart jump.

"*Allá está*," Marty said, pointing a thick, tattooed finger toward a tiny boat heading for shore.

They pulled off on a rutted dirt road cutting between stunted trees frozen in windblown poses. They jounced down a steep slope, the tires skidding

201

and brush scraping the side of the car. "Slow down, *wey*," Isaias said. "This road *es puro puto.*"

Marty slowed a little, and Riel's grip on the edge of her seat loosened slightly. They got to the bottom of the slope and parked on the edge of the dunes.

Riel hugged herself as both men got out of the car. Then Isaias came around and opened her door. His pistol was in his hand. "Get out."

Riel crawled out, her legs numb, a gusty, salt-scented breeze tangling her already messy hair. Isaias laid a hand on her shoulder, shoving the barrel of the gun in the curve of her back. "Go," he said, marching her forward.

They followed a faint path through the dunes, dunegrass whipping against her legs. The sand was cold on her bare feet, and every so often she'd step on a sharp rock or exposed root and stumble, which made Isaias hiss and grip her shoulder harder, jabbing her with the gun. A brackish pond spread across the path in the midst of the dunes, and they splashed through it, the water soaking Riel's pajama pants as she sank to the ankles in the squishy mud. Behind them, she heard Marty curse.

"I'm gonna lose a shoe in this *pinche* quicksand, *wey*," he said.

"It sucks you down, I'll throw you a vine, like Tarzan," Isaias said, and the men snickered. Riel blinked back tears, feeling incredibly alone.

Then they came around the last of the dunes, and the deep roar of the ocean hit their ears. There was a large speedboat moored beyond the swells, and three men were unloading packages from a dinghy beached nearby. One of the guys waved at them.

Isaias nudged Riel with the pistol barrel, and they trudged through the soft sand, stepping over piles of driftwood.

"I'm gonna put this gun up to avoid drama," Isaias said in her ear, "but you try anything, it comes out again, and I can almost guarantee you'll get shot in the confusion."

Riel nodded. The pressure of the gun disappeared from her back, and she glanced around at the dunes and open beach, wondering if there were agents hidden anywhere, or if she were on her own. She felt suddenly small, a little girl caught amongst violent men out here on this vast, windblown stretch of beach.

The men at the dinghy stopped unloading as the trio approached, and stood by the pile of packages on the dry sand. The bricks were wrapped in white plastic and stacked in a rough pyramid about three feet high. Riel's heart thumped. That was a *lot* of drugs. She wondered if they were real, and supposed they must be—not all of these men could be in on the government double-cross.

In fact, she was probably the only one here who knew. She swallowed hard.

One of the men, short and round with thinning hair, smiled as he wiped the sand off his hands and held one out to Isaias. His eyes lingered on Riel. "You guys must be Isaias and Marty," he said, clasping hands with both men. "And this one must be the girl I've been hearing about." He grinned wider.

"This is my girl, Riel," Isaias said, his hand tightening on her shoulder.

The man took Riel's hand in both of his, which were damp and calloused. "*Mucho gusto*, Riel," he said. "I'm Rolo."

She nodded, forcing a smile. "Nice to meet you."

The two men behind Rolo stared at her. Then one of the guys said something in a low voice, which Riel couldn't hear over the roar of the ocean, and they all snickered. Heat rose to her cheeks, and she stared out to sea to hide her expression. Would Isaias try to sell her to these men, or others like them? Her stomach churned and she pressed her hands to her belly, fighting off nausea.

The men exchanged a few words as Marty handed over the money. One of the men put the bag of cash in the dinghy, pushed the boat into the waves, and motored out towards the moored speedboat. The rest of them picked up the packages and started hauling them back over the dunes to the Impala.

Riel shoved a brick under each arm and accompanied the group down the sandy path, her scalp tingling and ears ringing. She tensed every time they passed a rise, imagining federal gunmen behind it, but all they encountered were chipmunks and a great blue heron in the marsh that almost gave Riel a heart attack when it took flight, beating its long, thin wings against the blustery air.

They found the car just as they'd left it. No one else was in sight. Riel watched the line of stunted trees, which stood like sentinels, for any signs of movement. Marty removed the hidden panels and loaded the drugs into the car's secret compartments. She jumped slightly when a raven flew, croaking, from the trees. She caught Isaias glancing at her suspiciously and forced her gaze to her feet.

Rolo and his friend made admiring comments about the Impala and its modifications. Sweat trickled down Riel's spine despite the breeze, and her shoulder muscles felt like they were about to snap.

They had to return to the beach for the rest of the packages. Riel's feet were now caked with mud and blood from walking barefoot, her pajama bottoms flopping wetly around her ankles. Still no one appeared to arrest them. Her heart began to flutter in her chest, and the packages under her arms slipped against her sweaty skin. In the depths of her mind, the certainty grew that there was no way the feds would have been able to keep up with all the changes in plans. That's why they'd given her the phone and earrings in the first place, and she'd been stupid enough to leave them behind. If she'd had the earrings, then she might have at least been able to give them clues about their location. She cursed herself for taking them off the night before, but they were so bulky and had poked her jaw and kept her awake.

After they loaded the final package, the men shook hands, and Rolo clasped her hand again. "I hope we see each other again soon," he said.

She smiled. "Me too." *In a perp lineup, with me identifying you from behind a one-way mirror.*

Rolo and his friend retreated, their backs disappearing behind a rise in the dunes.

"I'll drive," Isaias said.

Marty raised his eyebrows. "Really?"

"Yeah," Isaias said, and Riel flinched as he clasped her shoulder. "I'm tired of looking after this bitch. It's your turn." He pushed her roughly into the backseat and shut the door.

The two men climbed in. Marty gave her an odd glance, but she barely had the energy to wonder about it. Isaias started the car and headed back up the slope into the trees. He had to gun the engine in order to make it up the steep incline; the undercarriage grated against rocks and the tires slipped in several places. "*Chingada madre,*" he muttered, his hands tight on the wheel.

"This car wasn't made for this type of run," Marty said, trying to see the tires out his side window.

"The other place, the road wasn't like this," Isaias said. "But this place is actually less sketchy, not as many people."

Finally, the car lurched to the top of the slope, the tires catching on the even ground and jolting them forward. Isaias and Marty heaved a sigh of relief, but Riel dug her fingernails into the leather upholstery even harder. What if she wasn't able to escape before Isaias took her to wherever he had planned? Would she be willing to play the game, fuck him and pretend to like him in order to stay alive?

She swallowed hard. She wasn't sure she could.

She stared out the window at the lichen-draped branches, wondering if it wouldn't be easier to die. Would it hurt, if she provoked him to shoot her? What if he didn't get her in the head, or somewhere else where it would be quick? What if she ended up shot in the gut and died slowly?

She was jerked out of her morbid thoughts by Isaias' panicked yell. "Fuck!"

Riel blinked, her spine jerking straight.

"Holy shit!" Marty said.

Isaias slammed on the brakes.

Chapter Nineteen

The Impala's tires scraped to a stop in the dirt, Riel's seatbelt locking and jolting her against her seat.

They were at the junction where the dirt road met the pavement, and their way was blocked by half a dozen cars. Riel felt scores of guns and rifles pointed at her before her brain registered the image. Police wearing flack jackets were leaning over the tops of unmarked sedans and SUVs, more creeping out of the trees beside and behind them. She gulped a mouthful of air.

"*Que gran putas?*" Isaias hissed. He slammed the car into park and pulled his gun. Marty pulled his as well, holding it low over the dash.

Marty's and Isaias' necks twisted around, taking in the scene. Isaias' eyes flashed with panic; Marty's were hard and wary.

Someone nearby spoke into a bullhorn. "You're completely surrounded. Put down your guns and exit the car slowly with your hands up."

Isaias' lips pulled back over his clenched teeth,

and he lunged between the seats, grabbing a fistful of Riel's hair. She screeched as he pulled her into a sloppy headlock. She struggled against him and got tangled in the seatbelt as she felt the cold steel of a gun barrel being pressed to the crown of her head.

"This is your fault," he said. "You did this. I'll fucking kill you, you goddamn slut." Riel screamed again, kicking against the door, and he hit her hard over the head with the pistol.

"No, brother," Marty said, as fireworks went off inside Riel's skull. "Leave her be. You'll just make this worse."

"Fuck you," Isaias hissed, tightening his headlock.

Marty grasped Isaias' shoulder. "No, Isaias. We've got bigger worries now. Leave it. Leave her alone."

Riel stopped struggling. For a moment, Isaias hesitated, his arm tight around her throat, his jaw twitching, the gun barrel biting into her scalp. He cursed. Isaias let Riel go, shoving her back against the seat, where she lay quietly, breathing hard.

"Fuck," he spat, staring out the windshield at the bristling circle of gunmen closing in around them. Riel could see two approaching her side and lay very still, watching them closely.

Isaias' mouth drew into a tight line. He put the gun in his lap and slammed the car back into gear. Riel gasped as he stomped on the accelerator, the seatbelt cutting into her chest as he jerked the wheel, driving over the shallow ditch beside the road.

"What the hell!" Marty yelled.

Two gunmen had to dive out of the way as the car barreled toward them, Isaias jerking the wheel hard to navigate between the trunks of the stunted pines. Riel ducked instinctively, and her eyes met Marty's, who was crouched behind the glove box. They exchanged a look of terror for a split second before there was a confusion of gunshots and breaking glass and yells and cursing in the car. Riel threw her hands over her head. The windshield shattered and fell in chunks onto the dashboard. Something hit her head and she yelped before she realized it was tempered glass from the back window, which had also shattered.

"Fuck, I can't see," Isaias said, punching at one of the holes in the windshield and widening it. He jerked the wheel hard to avoid hitting a tree. There were more gunshots from the cops, and Riel cowered with her head between her knees, wondering what it would feel like to be hit by a bullet. Would she even feel it at all? Or would she just be…gone?

There was a heavy lurch, and for a moment Riel thought the car had been hit, or had run into something. But then their ride smoothed out, the tires hissed on the pavement; they'd come over the embankment and onto the road.

"What are you doing?" Marty yelled. "You can't outrun them!"

"I can sure as fuck try." Isaias floored it, slamming it into second and then third, the engine bellowing. The wind hissed through the broken windshield and caused more chunks of tempered glass to cascade onto the dashboard. The hole in the

210

back window made an eerie howl.

"You're fucking *chiflado, wey*," Marty said.

"I'm not just laying down for these assholes."

Marty wiped his forehead. "We're gonna get killed." He said it with a sort of surprised certainty, as if announcing they'd get *carnitas* for dinner, and Riel's chest tightened; he was probably right. The FBI wouldn't worry about keeping her or anyone in the car alive in this sort of situation.

The sound of sirens started up behind them. Isaias took a curve at full speed, the tires screeching. Another chunk of the windshield fell, the pieces skittering over the dash and sliding onto the floor. Riel put her head back between her knees, biting her tongue. *After all that shit, I'm going to die anyway.*

"Watch out!" Marty yelled, and Riel was thrown sideways into the door as Isaias swerved hard. Her neck snapped up just in time to see a car barreling toward them off of the shoulder, missing the passenger door by inches.

"Fucking fuckers," Isaias said.

"They're gonna have people all along this road, brother," Marty said, his voice shaking. "Just pull over. Just give up or we're gonna be killed. There's always a way out of prison, but no way out if you're dead."

"Better to die like a warrior than live like a *panocha*," Isaias said. "Stop sitting there like an old turd and shoot out their tires. I know a back way if we can dump them."

The sirens were closer now. Riel risked a glance back and saw two sheriffs' cars and an unmarked

SUV swinging around the last corner.

"Shit," Marty said quietly. He passed his hand over his grey face. Then he rolled down the window.

He turned in his seat, squinting back at their pursuers. Then he fired three shots before quickly pulling his arm back inside.

There was a burst of return fire. Riel clutched herself, but none of the shots hit the car.

"I fucking missed them," Marty muttered. "It's a hard shot."

"Try again!"

Marty's nostrils flared as he looked back at their pursuers. Riel could see beads of sweat on his pallid forehead. He heaved a sigh and raised his arm again, aiming out the window.

Just as he fired, there was a loud noise under the car and it began to swerve wildly. Riel screamed; Isaias cursed and grappled with the wheel.

"Those goddamn nail strips!" Isaias said. "Shit!"

There was another bang, and they skidded off the road, crashing over a small embankment and coming to rest on the shoulder. The engine shuddered to a stop.

"I missed their tires, but they got ours," Marty said weakly.

Cop cars pulled up on either side of them, and the SUV behind. The sirens quit. Men poured out, aiming their weapons. Riel's cheeks felt cold; she realized they were wet.

"Put your guns down and step out of the car!" a voice bellowed through a bullhorn. "Now!"

Riel was shaking hard. She unbuckled her

seatbelt, so eager to climb out of the car and surrender that she didn't notice Isaias' arm come back until it was already around her throat.

She screamed hoarsely and struggled, and he dove between the seats, catching her in a headlock again. She felt a sharp blow to the back of her head, and then the pistol barrel being pressed to her temple. Isaias' fingernails dug hard into her shoulder. "Fuck off and stop kicking, Riel!"

She tried to go still, but she was trembling so badly that her body still twitched away from him of its own accord. Isaias' fingernails dug deeper into her skin. He jerked her roughly through the gap between the seats. Her hip banged hard against the center console, and she fell with her left shoulder in Isaias' lap, the gun still jabbed into her skull.

"If you shoot, the girl gets hit too!" Isaias yelled, his voice painfully loud in the confined cabin. "She's your little bitch who set this shit up, right?" His fist came up, and he brought it down hard on her waist, pounding her once, twice, three times. Riel squirmed, trying to avoid the blows, but couldn't.

"Fucking stop it, Isaias!" Marty said, grasping his arm. "What are you doing? Just leave her alone."

"Fucking cunt," Isaias muttered. "I should have fucking unloaded a clip into your pussy the moment I saw you."

"Relax, Mr. Mendez," the voice speaking through the bullhorn said. "There's no need to make this situation more complicated than it already is."

"I'll tie your goddamn dicks in knots," Isaias

213

said. "How's that for complicated?" Riel yelled in pain as he pulled her completely over the console and into his lap, wrenching her hip and arm, jabbing her elbow and belly into the stick shift. The steering wheel dug into her back. Marty cursed as she accidentally kicked him. She went still, cramped and shaking, the cold steel of the gun barrel stinging the skin below her ear. Sweat ran into her eyes, and her mouth was full of her own hair.

"We're coming out," Isaias yelled. "You try anything, Riel dies."

"Okay, this shit needs to stop," Marty said quietly.

Riel felt Isaias go very still. "What the fuck, *hermano*?" he muttered. There was a tinge of panic in his voice.

Riel looked through her tangle of hair and saw Marty had his pistol to Isaias' head. "Put your gun down, Isaias."

Isaias' grip on Riel's arm tightened enough to make her flinch. "What, you're in on this too?"

"They made me an offer," Marty said. "I had to look after my own interests. Sorry, brother."

"But you were fucking shooting at them!"

"If I'd meant to hit them, I would have."

"*Fuck,*" Isaias said. "*Que vayas mucho a la puta chingada.*"

There was a brief struggle, then a deafening gunshot. Riel cowered. As the pressure slowly cleared from her ears, she realized she was still alive. There was something wet on her face. She saw blood splattered all over the windshield.

She twisted her neck around. Isaias' face was

grey and splattered in blood, and he was looking over at the passenger seat with tight lips, his chest heaving. Riel made herself look where Isaias was looking.

Marty was slumped against the car door, and where his face had been was a mass of blood and flesh, the white gleam of broken teeth.

She screamed. She closed her eyes, but the image was burned into her brain. She screamed again, and only stopped because she couldn't get enough air.

"Shut up!" Isaias said. He punched her arm over and over, then she flinched as the hot gun barrel burned her temple. "Fuck off, Riel, and stop with that fucking wailing."

She lay there in silence, breathing hard, not feeling the cramped and contorted position of her body.

"We're getting out of this fucking car, and just do what I tell you, or you'll end up like that fucking *chimosa*."

Her guts flooded with sickness. The image of the thing sitting in the next seat flashed in her mind, over and over. She nodded, whimpering.

"Back off the car!" Isaias yelled. "We're coming out, and if anyone makes a move, I kill this cunt immediately."

Riel's heart beat against her ribcage.

"Open the door," Isaias ordered her, his voice unsteady. "You go first. You try to run, I shoot you. You'd better hope your friends out there care about your worthless life, or you'll end up shot, anyway."

"Okay, okay," Riel said, slightly surprised she

215

could still speak, "but I have to twist around, Isaias. I don't have room. I can't reach the door."

"Twist around then."

She jabbed him with her knees trying to turn her body, and she cringed as she felt her ankle brush against Marty's warm, inert flesh. She got her hand on the door handle and pulled, sliding sideways as the door opened. Isaias caught her by the shoulder so she didn't fall out. "Crawl out and put your feet on the ground, that's it," he murmured.

She dragged herself out onto the damp forest floor, which smelled good, like earth and pine needles. Sickness rose up inside her and she vomited into the cool loam.

"Get up, Riel!" Isaias yelled.

She heaved again and again and took a deep breath, then eased herself into a standing position, her legs shaking. Facing her, not five feet away, next to one of the sheriff's cars, was a man in a bullet-proof vest, a handgun pointed directly at her. His eyes glittered alertly, meeting hers. On either side, two more officers pointed two more guns.

"Don't move," Isaias said. She heard him get out behind her. She was still staring at the man with the gun, who didn't give her any sign or signal. Would they even care if she died? She'd played her part already, they didn't need her anymore. A dull wave of hopelessness flooded her guts. She felt like no one had ever been able to protect her her whole life, and now that short life was about to end. Either Isaias would shoot her, or the cops would, trying to shoot Isaias.

She felt the barrel of Isaias' pistol nestle itself

between her shoulder blades.

"Back off!" he yelled. "I want all of you away from the car. Do it now or she dies! You don't want your fucking precious cunt snitch to die, do you?"

For a moment, no one moved. Then, to Riel's surprise, the gunmen began to back off.

"Put your guns down," Isaias said.

"Mr. Mendez, let's try to find a way to resolve this without anyone else getting hurt," the same voice said through the bullhorn. Riel could see its owner now, a tall thin guy standing half-hidden behind the SUV. "If you put your gun down now, we can figure this out, okay?"

The pistol barrel jabbed her hard. "Stop standing around fiddling with your limp dicks and figure it out yourself." He wrapped his hand in her tangled hair and jerked so that Riel found herself looking up at the blue sky and the silvery popcorn puffs of a cumulous cloud. She blinked, an irrational feeling of peace spreading through her.

"Put your guns down, or I'll shoot this bitch now!" Isaias said.

Riel couldn't see what was going on, but she heard a shuffling amongst the crowd of police. Were they really putting their guns down? Her brow furrowed.

"Okay, now clear off," Isaias said. She heard more shuffling, and he poked her again with the gun. "Walk, Riel."

She stumbled forward, her head still pulled back so she was staring up. She placed her feet unsteadily on the uneven ground, but Isaias pushed her onward with the relentless pressure of the gun. Tree branches covered the sky as they entered the forest. She couldn't believe the cops were really just going to let them walk off into the woods.

"Isaias, where are we going?" She tripped over something and almost fell. He yanked her back up by her hair, making her yelp.

"Let me worry about that, Rielita." His voice sounded odd, his breathing rasping heavily.

She stumbled again, and he yanked her hair harder, bringing tears to her eyes. "Goddammit, Isaias, let my fucking hair go. I can't see where I'm going."

"I don't want you to fucking see where you're going."

She tripped over what felt like a rock and almost fell again. They were walking slowly; she could still hear the cops' radios behind them. Weren't they even going to follow? "I'm not going to run off, Isaias! Where would I go? You'd shoot me, or the cops would."

"The cops aren't going to shoot their precious little snitch bitch."

Riel swallowed the bile that rose back up in her throat. "You already shot the snitch, Isaias. Weren't you paying attention?"

"You two were in it together, conspiring like little rats in a cage."

"No, Isaias! I'd never met him before today. Please..."

"Fucking lying twat!" he yelled.

He yanked her hair so hard she felt some of it tear from her scalp. Then he punched her on the side of the head, the blow thudding dully in her ears.

She stumbled forward. Her knees buckled, and she went down hard, her forehead cracking sharply against a rock.

There were gunshots. Riel, her head swimming and her vision blurred with pain, cowered in the dirt.

The gunshots stopped. For a moment, all she could hear was a ringing in her ears, the beating of her heart. The noise of it seemed distant, her mind floating away in a haze.

She raised her head and looked back toward Isaias. He still held the gun, but he held it limply, not aiming it. He had a vaguely surprised, almost peaceful look.

A scream rose up in Riel's throat, but all that came out was a pitiful moan. Blood welled up, soaking Isaias' shirt. The gun dropped from his slack fingers. His eyes went blank and he fell to the ground, like a marionette whose strings had been cut.

Riel threw up again, vomit spewing from her mouth and splattering her hands and chest. Then she fell too, collapsing back onto the earth. She stared, bemused, at a pink mushroom poking through the dirt in front of her face. It was the last thing she saw before darkness swallowed her.

Chapter Twenty

The pain in her head was what brought her back, pulling her cruelly through the leagues of empty forgetfulness.

Her skull pounded with white hot light. Her mouth was dry and her stomach seemed to be struggling to escape her body.

She lay very still. There were voices around her, and a confusion of noise. Her head and stomach hurt worse when she tried to make sense of it. Fear zinged through her; she was still with Isaias, she needed to escape.

Then she remembered: he was shot. He fell. Or had that been a dream?

She opened her eyes, squinting at the bright light. She quickly closed them again, dizziness catching her up in its riptide.

"Riel!" a voice said. She felt a cold hand take hers.

She cracked her eyes open again, and Lizette's face swam in front of them, her eyes tear-streaked and full of anguish, one of them purple and swollen shut.

Relief flooded her, mixing with the pain, and Riel tried to smile. "You're alive," she said.

Lizette laughed, more tears escaping her good eye. "Of course I'm alive. *You're* the one in the hospital. Oh my God, Riel."

Lizette pressed her cheek to Riel's chest, clasping her in an awkward hug, shaking with sobs.

"You're alive," Riel repeated weakly. Then her headache and nausea surged back, pulling her again into the depths of unconsciousness.

***

Riel had confused dreams.

She was following Isaias down a dirt trail edged by trees and shacks of rough-hewn wood. Her feet crunched on empty potato chip bags, which lay on the ground, ankle-deep.

"Hurry up, Riel, Evan's waiting."

He turned off the trail towards one of the shacks and opened the door, standing aside for her to go in.

She stepped through the doorway into a dim, dirt-floored room. On the ground, crumpled on a heap of trash, was a man. His arms and legs were sprawled awkwardly, his face hidden in shadow.

Riel felt a pang of sickness. She recognized those shoes, the shape of those legs. She stepped forward.

"No," she said. The ground seemed to drop out from under her feet. Where Evan's face had been, there was now only a mass of splattered flesh,

221

broken teeth.

***

She awoke with a gasp, reality seeping into her mind as the dream drained out.

She was dizzy. Her head still ached, but not badly. The light was too bright, and there was too much furniture in the room, tubes and wires and electronic boxes...

"Auntie Riel!"

She remembered. She was in a hospital bed. Olivia rushed to her side, burying her face in her chest, which was covered by a flannel gown.

"Olivia," Riel said, her voice croaky. She lifted her arm to put it around the little girl, but stopped when she felt a sharp tug; an IV was inserted into her vein, the tube tangled in the blankets. She let her arm fall back to her side. "Olivia, I missed you so much," she said.

Others stood at the foot of the bed: Lizette, Laina, and Robert. Robert had his arm around Laina, who was bouncing Riel's baby niece Corinne on her hip, and holding three-year-old Jessica's hand.

Riel fought back a rush of fear. Evan wasn't there. *Maybe he hasn't had time to get here yet.*

Laina smiled and came over to kiss Riel on the forehead. Corinne grinned toothlessly and reached out a chubby hand toward Riel's face. Jessica hung back, her brown eyes wide, her fingers in her mouth.

"You're awake," Laina said.

Riel smiled. Her face felt stiff and sore, and smiling felt strange. "Laina, you're here," she said.

"Of course I am." Her ice-blue eyes examined Riel; they weren't cold any longer, but full of pity and pride. "You're so brave," she murmured.

"What happened to me?" Riel asked. "Why am I here?"

"You have a concussion," Laina said. "They don't think it's that bad, but they think you're suffering from shock and exhaustion too, which is understandable, given what happened..."

Laina trailed off, her eyes searching Riel's face.

"How long have I been out?" Riel murmured.

"Just a few hours," Lizette said.

Riel let out a breath. Evan couldn't have gotten here that quickly, could he?

Olivia still had her face pressed into Riel's armpit. She was sniffling, her small shoulders trembling, and Riel winced. She was being selfish, thinking about Evan right now. Her eyes found her sister's; the left one looked even worse now than she'd seen the first time she woke up—black and green, just a slit of eye shining under the swollen lid. Lizette's right eye was dull and bloodshot. "I'm so sorry," Riel said. "I didn't mean for it to end like that, Lizette."

Her sister put her hands to her face. Laina and Robert exchanged a look, then Laina smiled and put a hand on Olivia's shoulder.

"Come on, sweet thang, let's go get some ice cream in the cafeteria."

Olivia glanced between Laina and Riel.

"I'll still be awake when you come back," Riel

223

said. "Go get some ice cream, and help Laina pick out a treat for me too."

Olivia brightened a bit. "I'll get you some tamarind candy. That's your favorite."

Riel smiled. "If they have it. Otherwise, chocolate is okay."

They all filed out of the room, leaving Riel to gaze at her trembling sister. Lizette took her hands from her face, her good eye even redder now. "I know you didn't mean for him to die, Riel. And you did the right thing. You really did. It's just…"

"I know," Riel said, her dried-out eyeballs stinging with tears.

"He wasn't a good husband to me," Lizette said huskily. "I know that. But there were good things about him too, deep down. He just got so caught up in this business."

"I know," Riel said again, tears spilling over.

Lizette pushed a chair over to the bedside and sat, clasping Riel's hand, pressing it to her wet cheek. "I love you, sister," she said. "I know you did what you did partially to save me and the kids. I know it was you who had him give me the money. He never would have done that on his own."

Riel's heart jumped. She'd forgotten all about the money. Would there still be an investigation now? "Did you get it transferred? Or did he stop you first?"

Lizette sat up, sniffing. "I got it transferred. He was so angry…it was scary…I was sure he was going to kill you."

Riel let out a breath. "I thought he was going to kill *you.*"

Lizette's hand crept up to gingerly touch her black eye. "He wouldn't have killed me. But you…you should have heard the things he said…"

"He would have killed me eventually, I think," Riel murmured. Another wave of nausea took her, and she sat very still until it passed. "He didn't have any problem killing people. He killed Marty when he found out he was working with the police, and they seemed to be good friends." Riel swallowed hard. She hadn't even known Marty, but he'd probably saved her life. Why hadn't the police even told her he was one of theirs?

Lizette blinked, carefully wiping her swollen eye with a wadded tissue. "You mean the guy in the car with you guys, right?"

Riel nodded.

"He didn't die. He'll be all scarred up, but they saved him."

The image of Marty's torn-apart face flashed unwillingly across her mind. It had looked like he'd been destroyed. She swallowed hard. "Really?"

Lizette nodded, wiping her eyes again. "When the cops came to arrest Mama Maria, a guy named Officer Norton came with them. After they asked me a bunch of questions, he told me everything that happened."

All the air went out of Riel, dread creeping in. "Officer Norton was here? Was Evan with him?"

Lizette's brow furrowed slightly. "No. Should he have been?" She looked at Riel searchingly, and a slight, teasing smile flitted over her lips. "Are you two together now?"

Riel twisted the scratchy sheet between her

fingers. "I guess so." But then why wasn't he here? If Norton had time to get here, Evan should have been here too.

A grin briefly overtook the pain on Lizette's face. "That's good. I always liked Evan." Then the smile faded again, her gaze dropping to her lap.

Riel squeezed her sister's hand. "I'm glad you're okay, Lizette."

Lizette scooted closer. Riel put her arm around her shoulders the best she could, trying not to tangle the IV lines.

They were sitting there like that when a man in a white coat strode into the room, introducing himself as Dr. Rogers. He checked Riel's monitors. Then he shone a penlight into her eyes and asked a bunch of questions, testing her memory and focus.

When he was done, he smiled and removed her IV, pressing a wad of cotton to the puncture and gently taping it up. "You had a bang to the head, and I think you sustained a concussion, but I don't think I need a CT scan. You're recovering nicely. I'd like to keep you overnight for observation because of your loss of consciousness, but if all goes well you'll be discharged tomorrow."

Riel thanked him. He stepped out, and Laina and the others filed back in.

They sat and talked about nothing for a while, trying to clear the atmosphere, but Riel chewed her lip, worrying about Evan. Every time someone walked past her room, her heart leapt, but it was never him. Had something happened to him? Or had he just had time to change his mind about her?

The sunlight through the windows began to turn

ruddy and fade. Eventually, Riel's visitors stood up to leave. Lizette kissed her forehead, Laina fussed with her covers, and Olivia buried her face in her neck.

"You going to be all right?" Laina asked. "You're pale. I think you might need more rest."

"I'll be fine," Riel said, trying to smile.

Lizette frowned. "Are you sure?"

Riel examined her sister's bruised and unhappy face. "It's you I'm worried about, Lizette."

Her sister grimaced, then winced, her hand coming up to her bruised eye. "I'll be okay. Laina and Robert are staying over with me tonight." She gave Riel one last kiss on the forehead. "I'll be back tomorrow to pick you up."

They left, and Riel was alone with her thoughts. She stared out the darkening windows, biting the inside of her cheek. She tried to make excuses for Evan not being there, but none of them were good enough to ease her nagging worry, anger, and hurt.

Despite this, her eyes kept drifting closed. Riel couldn't remember ever feeling so exhausted. Eventually, her fatigue took over and she fell asleep.

She had vivid, confused dreams of searching for Evan, something always sidetracking her so that she arrived where he'd been moments after he'd left. Then she found out he was sneaking behind her back and having an affair with Mama Maria.

A noise pulled her back into reality and wakefulness. She opened her eyes, blinking. It was a moment before the world wavered into focus and she remembered where she was.

She jumped as someone took her hand. Then she looked over and gasped.

Evan was standing at her bedside, looking pale, dark circles ringing his eyes. But then he smiled, and his face lit up, dispelling the tired look.

"Evan," she breathed.

"Riel I'm so freakin' glad you're okay." He leaned over and kissed her, a slow kiss, his fingertips brushing the curve of her neck. "Oh, Riel, God, I'm so glad."

He kissed her again. Riel felt her tension melt away at the touch of his lips, his hand sliding down to her waist, but she tore herself away, pushing him back.

"Where have you been? Norton was here, and everyone else. Did you have other appointments or something? Did your car break down?"

His mouth tightened. "No, Riel. The damn cops wouldn't let me go."

Her retort died on her lips. "Huh?"

"They were worried about retaliation by Isaias' people. They held me for hours, no matter how much I yelled at them that no one was going to defend that fuckhole's honor. Finally I got an escort here. You have guards too, you know."

"No, I didn't know. But nothing's happened? None of Isaias' people have tried anything?"

Evan shook his head. "Nothing."

Riel sighed, her eyes closing. Was it really over? She knew she'd be reliving the previous day for the rest of her life, seeing Marty's blown-apart face, and the image of Isaias' last expression as he fell to the ground, for years, probably. But if she really didn't have to keep looking over her shoulder, waiting for the gunshot that would end her quiet life, proving once and for all that no one could escape the world of drugs and gangs—if she, Evan, and her family were really safe now, then it had all been worth it.

She opened her eyes, seeing Evan's handsome and worried face, and smiled. "So I guess we can go live down south now, and pretend we're regular people."

A faint smile flitted across his lips. "We are regular people, Riel. Regular people with a past, maybe, but everyone has a past. That's why they call it a *past*. Because it's over with."

Riel interlaced her fingers with Evan's, pulling him toward her, kissing him again. "I'm sorry I yelled," she murmured.

"It's okay. Totally understandable." He pressed his lips against her neck, his hand finding its way under the tightly-tucked sheets, blankets, and her hospital gown to caress her breasts. "It was hell being away from you, Riel. I was so worried. I can't believe how much shit they made you go through. Norton told me the whole story, and I wanted to fucking punch him."

"It's okay, it's over now." She sighed as his hands slid down her belly.

"I missed you so goddamn much. I thought I was going to go crazy." His lips met hers again, hungrily, and she drew a breath as his gentle fingers found her clit. "I'm never letting you out of my sight again," he said, rubbing slowly. "That shit is over now forever. Our new life starts right now."

"I love you, Evan," she gasped, pressing against his hand.

"I love you too, Riel."

She sighed in disappointment as he took his fingers away. "Don't tease me," she said, giving him a pouty look.

He laughed, then snuck over and closed the door. He pulled the privacy curtain around the bed for good measure, then he crawled up next to her on the narrow cot. Riel scooted over against the sidebars to accommodate him.

She ran her finger lightly over his bandaged shoulder. "It doesn't hurt you, to be like this?"

"I'm fine. I barely feel it. You? How's your head? You hurting?"

She smiled. "I feel just fine, now that you're here."

He kissed her, his lips and tongue lingering on hers, his hands caressing her body and pulling her against him. Riel ran her hands up his shirt, feeling the muscles of his chest. The warmth of his body and the sweetness of his lips engulfed her, driving out all her pain and worries, making her feel whole. She interlaced her legs with his, wanting every inch of her skin against his.

He pushed up her hospital gown, squeezing her breasts, his lips working their way down her jaw, her neck, to her nipples. Riel closed her eyes, sighing, as he laid kisses down her belly. His lips made their way to her navel, then went lower, his breath warm against her skin. He tugged her panties down over her hips, and she wiggled out of them, tossing them aside. He looked up at her, his eyes lingering on her body.

"You're so beautiful, even in that nasty hospital gown." He pushed her thighs apart, leaning down to push his tongue inside her.

Riel bit her lip to keep herself from crying out, pressing her hips up against his mouth. He stroked her clit with two fingers, his tongue slowly exploring.

"Evan, I want you," she moaned, and he made a muffled noise. "Evan, fuck me, please." He pressed harder with his fingers, fucking her slow with his tongue, pleasure building up inside her. "Please, Evan."

Finally, he sat up, pulling his jeans down his hips. Riel grasped his shoulders and flipped him over on his back, lifting up her gown and straddling him.

She sighed and he moaned as she slowly lowered herself down onto his hard cock. She watched as his green eyes glazed over with need, feeling that same need in herself. "Oh, Riel," he said, breathing heavily.

He grabbed her ass and moved inside her as she rode him, slowly, taking him as deep as she could. He leaned up to take each of her nipples into his hot mouth.

She felt the head of his cock moving deep in her, felt the heat growing. He moved faster, urgently, thrusting up into her. Then he gasped and moaned her name, his hips moving uncontrollably. She cried out as the pleasure took her over, filling every part of her.

Then she sat atop him, catching her breath. He

blinked up at her with a sly smile, and she suddenly remembered where they were.

"The doctor is going to kick me out if he finds us like this," Evan said.

Riel giggled. "I won't let him. You're good medicine." She crawled off him and cuddled against him in the narrow bed, careful not to jostle his bad shoulder. He pulled the blanket over the both of them and they lay there holding each other, their legs entwined.

"I want to be with you forever, Riel," he said, and she smiled.

"I'd like that a lot."

Chapter Twenty-One

Six Months Later…

Evan came in and hung his work hat on the hook beside the door. "Hey, Rielita," he said, pressing his lips to her neck. "Studying again?"

She wrinkled her nose at the books spread out on the dining table. "Yeah. I just realized I have a test on Monday, and I'm not ready at all. I don't know why I have to take all this math. It's killing me."

He laughed, gently ruffling her hair. "You got an A on the last test, so don't complain, you nerd."

She grinned. "How was work?"

"Busy. I did about twenty estimates today."

"That's awesome. Business must be really good."

"It is. What's cooking? It smells awesome."

"I've got a chicken in the oven. Lizette is coming over with her new boyfriend."

Evan went into the kitchen and opened the oven door, gazing into it avidly, and Riel smiled to herself. He was always so excited about her home-cooked meals, even if she wasn't that good of a cook, and it felt good to feed him.

"Ah, we finally get to meet this famous boyfriend of hers, huh?" Evan said, staring at the baking chicken and rubbing his tummy absentmindedly.

"He'd better be nice, or I'll run him out of here. Close the oven, Evan, you're going to let all the heat out. Isn't our electrical bill high enough?"

He blew a raspberry and shut the oven, coming over to put his arms around her waist and nibble her ear. "Mishmash pays most of it, anyway."

"But still." An unwilling smile came to her face as he laid nibbling kisses along the curve of her neck, his hands wandering along her curves.

"Did you hear about Laina and Robert?" he muttered, kissing her breastbone.

"No, what?"

"They opened an Italian restaurant up in Portland. They're getting married in September."

Riel grinned wide, and turned in her chair to take him in her arms. "That's awesome."

"Mmmph," Evan said, sliding his fingers into the cup of her bra to pull her breast free. He sucked her nipple gently, and Riel's eyes fluttered closed as a wave of heat washed through her.

Evan took her hands and pulled her out of her chair, gently drawing her towards the bedroom. He gave her a hesitant glance.

"You know, we should get married."

Riel's steps faltered, and she blinked at him. "Really?"

He smiled uncertainly. "I mean, if you, you

234

know, want to."

She broke into a wide grin, her heart beating fast. She stood on her tiptoes, stretching up to kiss him. "Yes, I want to."

He wrapped his arms tight around her, his lips hot and passionate against hers.

Acknowledgments

I'd like to thank my parents; my husband, Eric; my daughter, Juniper; and the rest of my friends and family, especially my loyal cheering squad and counselors, Faith, Aleena, Mari, and Pastor Ivelisse. I know I'm a piece of work sometimes…all the time…but you guys have been there and have put up with it all.

I'd like to thank all my lovely critique groups and beta readers. You're all helping me to become a better writer, which is an intense and beautiful process.

I'd like to thank the great, hard-working people at Limitless Publishing for all their help, and for taking a chance on a writer like me.

I would also like to thank my Invisible Friend Jesus, who has on his Hollywood shades now and a brand new suit, quite proper for the savior of someone who would write a book like this.

And, of course, I'd like to thank Phoenix. I told you, curled up on your bathroom floor, that if you believed in something hard enough, it would come true. Well, they haven't bought any cinnamon rolls yet, but at least I'm in business.

About the Author

Elizabeth Roderick grew up as a barefoot ruffian on a fruit orchard near Yakima, in the eastern part of Washington State. After weathering the grunge revolution and devolution in Olympia, Washington, Portland, Oregon and Seattle, she recently moved to the (very, very) small town of Shandon, California: a small cluster of houses amidst the vineyards of the Central Coast.

She earned a bachelor's degree in Spanish from The Evergreen State College in Olympia, Washington, and worked for many years as a paralegal and translator. She went on to study chemistry, physics, and higher mathematics, with the goal of becoming a research chemist, but was eventually forced to concede that graduate school would require too much time away from her husband and daughter, and that–despite her good-enough grades –she was perhaps the wrong kind of nerd for such pursuits, being more the type that likes to dress in cloaks and hauberks rather than lab coats and goggles.

She is a musician and songwriter, and has played in many bands. She's rocked pretty much every instrument, including some she doesn't even know the real names for, but mostly guitar, bass and keyboards. She has two albums of her own, which you can listen to at pimentointhehole.com. She writes fiction novels for young adults and adults, as well as short stories, and keeps an active blog at: https://elizabethroderick.wordpress.com/.

Facebook:
https://www.facebook.com/elizabethroderickauthor

Twitter:
https://twitter.com/LidsRodney

Website:
https://elizabethroderick.wordpress.com/

Made in the USA
Monee, IL
10 June 2026

53029981R00142